STORM ON THE PLAINS

Numbly, Curtis thought of Fox Claw, out here somewhere riding through this same storm. Why didn't the Comanche quit? What was it that kept him going when he had no chance at all?

The cold fury of the storm cut Curtis's plans down to size. What did it matter? He almost hoped that Fox Claw would get away.

Run you fool! he thought. *Run and keep on running. Run and don't come back.*

But he knew that Fox Claw would not run forever.

The winter would be long, but not long enough.

The time for killing would come again. . . .

THE WOLF IS MY BROTHER

Chad Oliver

BANTAM BOOKS
TORONTO • NEW YORK • LONDON • SYDNEY • AUCKLAND

To J. Gilbert McAllister

This edition contains the complete text of the original hardcover edition.
NOT ONE WORD HAS BEEN OMITTED.

THE WOLF IS MY BROTHER
A Bantam Book / published by arrangement with the author

PRINTING HISTORY
Signet Books edition published January 1967
Bantam edition / September 1988

ISBN 0-553-27658-1

Published simultaneously in the United States and Canada

Bantam Books are published by Bantam Books, a division of Bantam Doubleday Dell Publishing Group, Inc. Its trademark, consisting of the words "Bantam Books" and the portrayal of a rooster, is Registered in U.S. Patent and Trademark Office and in other countries. Marca Registrada. Bantam Books, 666 Fifth Avenue, New York, New York 10103.

PRINTED IN THE UNITED STATES OF AMERICA

O 0 9 8 7 6 5 4 3 2 1

PART ONE

The Messiah
1874

Curtis

He sat tensely in his saddle, a tall man, his back rigid, his gray eyes restless and impatient. Waiting was hard for Curtis. He knew what was coming; it was his job to know. There weren't going to be any surprises. He knew the futile moves he could make and the effective moves he could not make. The inevitability of the situation bothered him, but he wanted to get on with it. He was wound up tight. He needed the release that action would bring to him.

Still, he waited. He had learned to wait.

He watched the buzzards riding the cold wind in the flat leaden sky. There were at least twenty of them, small with distance but sharply etched against the shapeless rain-swollen clouds. They wheeled and circled with a mindless fixity of purpose, quartering through the same sector of the sky, tied by invisible cords to something on the land below.

His eyes narrowed when he finally saw his scouting detail top the rise to the south. The men were riding hard.

Curtis shifted his weight in the McClellan saddle. The raw March wind funneled down out of the north and chilled his spine. He knew that wind. It was a living sheet of gray cold that moaned across the vast and treeless land, seeking him out. It snaked out of the frozen wastes of Canada, blew icily over the dark plains of the Sioux, whistled through the long empty miles and the lonely river valleys. It stirred the cold waters of the Platte, the Republican, the Arkansas, the Cimarron, and the Canadian, fifty miles away. It came after him. It had his name on it.

He could make out Lieutenant Pease now, riding just

ahead of Jim. Pease was still young enough to insist on leading; Jim would let him have his way as long as it made no real difference.

Curtis touched the sixteen-shot Henry .44 repeater in his saddle boot. It felt good. He wished that all of his men could have been equipped with the Henry. They said that it was a gun a man could load on Sunday and shoot all week. It wasn't that good, but it beat the breech-loading .45 caliber Springfields.

It didn't matter now. Curtis wasn't expecting a fight. He hadn't even ordered his men to take off their overcoats; it was too damned cold. He had sixty-five men in A Company, and there weren't that many Indians out in the whole Texas Panhandle.

Pease reined in his sorrel and saluted. His unlined face with its ambitious beard was pale under its patina of windburn.

"Well?" Curtis said.

"We found them, sir."

"How many?"

"Five. All dead."

Curtis glanced at the Tonkawa scout they all called Jim for the excellent reason that his Tonk name was an impossible jawbreaker. Old Jim, despite a slight addiction to cannibalism, was the best scout he had. If Jim said there were five dead men, then there were five dead men, no more and no less.

Jim nodded. "God damn," he said.

"Buffalo hunters?" Curtis asked Pease.

"They had two hide wagons with them, sir."

Curtis looked at Jim. "How long ago did it happen?"

Jim shrugged. "Two days. Maybe three." He paused. "God damn," he added, concluding his report.

"Any sign of Indians now?" Curtis asked.

"No, sir," Pease said. "They're long gone."

Curtis looked at Jim again. Jim said nothing. That meant that Pease was right. "We'll have a look. Lead the way, Pease." It did no harm to give Pease some authority now and then. Curtis turned to Captain Irvine, who had moved up on his bay. "Bring the men up slowly, will you,

Matt? We'll want to poke around a little before they trample things up."

Matt Irvine grinned and stroked his singularly unkempt moustache. "I'll get the burial detail ready. Got just the boys for the job."

Curtis nodded. Matt Irvine was a godsend. They had been together ever since Fort Wade was built, and he had yet to see Matt in a situation he couldn't handle. Matt had little imagination, but he had everything else.

"Let's go, Matt," he said.

Irvine waved the command forward.

Curtis rode easily, sensing the orderly movement of the troop behind him. He did not have to turn around to see the swallow-tailed guidon of A Company flying in the wind or the square blue regimental standard socketed in Trooper Rigney's right stirrup. He knew where every man was, and he knew what every man could do.

They rode under a close gray sky. The land was winter-barren in the cold of late March; the grass was a soggy gray-brown and the stunted mesquite trees were stark against the wind. There were puddles of black standing water in the hollows.

They climbed the rise and started down.

The buzzards sailed up the wind. They moved higher, but they did not go away.

They rode closer. Curtis eyed the two wagons, charred and dirty black against the brown of the dead grass. One wagon was on its side; stiff hides spilled from it, frozen in an illusion of motion. The other wagon was still upright. There was a dark scarecrow figure, upside down, fastened to one wheel.

He could just make out the rest of the bodies. They were very white and naked in the cold air. One of them was hanging halfway out of the upright wagon, the two hands almost touching the ground. Two others were stretched out side by side, neatly, just beyond the overturned wagon. The last body was some fifty yards away. It had been dragged around the wagons, many times. The trail it had made was still visible in the bent and broken grass.

Curtis dismounted and handed the reins to his striker. He walked stiffly down to the wagons.

Damned fools, he thought.

He remembered Phil Sheridan's speech in Austin. Little Phil had told the lawmakers to run off some medals for the buffalo hunters. The bronze medals were to have had a dead buffalo on one side and a discouraged Indian on the other.

Well, Little Phil's medals came high.

There wasn't much left of the man tied to the wagon wheel. The Indians had built a fire under his head. There must have been dry wood in the wagons; the buffalo chips had been too wet to burn. The other three nearby bodies had all been scalped, of course. Beyond that, it was hard to tell. The Indians had taken all of the clothing, just as they had taken the horses and mules and rifles. The swollen bodies were in bad shape. Maybe the Indians had done some of it, but the buzzards were not fastidious feeders and there were wolf or coyote tracks around.

It was too early for flies. That was something.

He picked his way through the litter—spilled coffee, sugar, and tobacco, mixed with strewn hides—and walked out to glance at the man who had been dragged. He turned away quickly and went back to the wagons.

The picture was clear enough. The hunters had been jumped as they slept, probably just at dawn. There had been a fight. Curtis counted seven spent metallic Sharps cartridges from the buffalo guns. The Indians must have taken some losses. They had carried their dead away with them, as always, but it must have been rough. There might have been twenty or thirty braves in the raiding party, but those odds weren't overwhelming and the Indians knew it. Most war parties wouldn't risk heavy losses in return for perhaps fifteen horses and mules. The Indians had cause to hate the buffalo hunters, but they were seldom reckless. Their idea was to hit and run, and a successful raiding party was one in which everyone got back alive to holler about his exploits.

Those five bodies meant that the Indians were getting desperate.

Curtis clamped his hat back on his head. He pulled out his pipe, filled it with Ridgewood tobacco, and lit it. The tang of the smoke helped. He walked around, looking for tracks in the spots that were bare of grass. There were not hard to find. The freshest ones had been made by Tonk moccasins—Jim and the other scouts with Pease. There were prints left by the boots of the buffalo hunters. And there were other moccasin tracks—plenty of them. There were some that he could not identify, but he would have bet his hole card that they were Kiowa. It wasn't much of a deduction; they were too far south for the Cheyenne, so they just about had to be Kiowa. There were others that he recognized at once. The tracks were short and stubby with the familiar fringe along the heel.

Comanche.

Curtis chewed on his pipe stem. The buffalo hunters had been south of the Arkansas, violating the Medicine Lodge treaty with their customary aplomb. The Comanches and the Kiowas were not supposed to be here either, but what could you expect? He was fairly certain that he knew where he could find them now. Unless they had hightailed it to join up with the Kwahadis out on the Staked Plains, which was unlikely, they were back on the reservation near Fort Sill in the Territory. That was a shade over one hundred miles away. With no infantry to slow him down, he could make that in three days. His A Company alone could handle the raiders.

Nevertheless, he could do exactly nothing.

What made it all the more galling was the fact that he didn't even have to go to Sill personally. John Davidson and the Tenth Cavalry were *stationed* at Sill. Davidson was in the same boat, of course; his hands were tied. Curtis knocked out his pipe on his muddy boot. Fighting Indians wasn't too tough, once you caught up with them. The real fight was with Reed and the other Quakers and the Indian Bureau and the Eastern newspapers that admired the Indians greatly from a vast, safe distance. If Sheridan and Sherman didn't get some backing from Grant soon, they might as well give this damned country back to the Comanches and Kiowas.

It was a crazy war, crazier than most.

He glanced around him. The rain-soaked land was utterly desolate. Mottled in dull colors, almost featureless beneath the gray banks of clouds, it rolled away to nowhere. The cold wind plucked at his coat.

He walked quickly back to the waiting men of A Company and motioned Matt Irvine to send in the burial detail. There was nothing more he could do.

He watched impatiently while the graves were dug. Once the hunters were buried, he moved out fast. He wanted to get away from the smell.

They got a break from the weather, with the clouds husbanding their considerable resources for a real gully-washer at a more inconvenient time. The outfit made twelve miles before nightfall. The evening mess was late, since the horses had to be attended to first, but the bugler sounded taps at nine as usual.

With any luck, they would ride into Wade tomorrow.

Curtis stepped outside his tent. The night was strangely hushed. A coyote yapped off to the west, sounding wet and miserable. That was the only sound except for the stirring of the horses and a slight hissing from the fire. It was an alien night, a shrouding night. It severed Curtis from the land, the land that was not his. He had ridden over this land, lived long years of his life on this land, but the land kept its distance. The land was the buffalo and the Comanche and the long, long winds. It was not white man's land, not yet.

Curtis knew that he was a stranger here, an intruder. Perhaps, he thought, the only real home we have is when we are very young. It had all changed in the War. Everything had changed, and himself most of all. He felt his muscles tightening. He did not want to think about the War again.

The cool night wrapped him in its silence. Comanche raiders rode at night, under the moon. It was bad medicine to start out on a raid in the daytime. There wasn't a person in Texas who could not recognize a Comanche moon.

Curtis did not hate the Indians, and he definitely did not fear them. He didn't quite know what he felt. Sometimes, when he saw them riding free under the huge blue sky, he almost envied them. Other times, when he watched the wrinkled squaws cutting up the beef on ration days at the reservation, he felt contempt for them. He felt disgust, revulsion, kinship, exasperation, wonder—all at different times. He knew they had gotten the short end of the stick, and it bothered him that he did not feel more strongly about it than he did.

The Indians meant something to him, of course. If there had been no Indians, there would have been few promotions. Promotions were hard enough to come by in this man's army, after the War. There were still plenty of gray-haired lieutenants kicking around.

He wasted no sympathy on the dead buffalo hunters. They had taken a chance and they had lost. That was all.

Colonel (Brevet Major General) William Foster Curtis, C.O. of the Twelfth Cavalry stationed at Fort Wade, turned in for the night. He closed his eyes and waited.

Sleep did not come at once. He was troubled by what he had seen that day. Not the bodies; they were nothing. But the blackened, charred wood of the wagons. The smoke-stained shredded canvas. The dirty burned spokes of the wagon wheel that held the cooked scarecrow figure. The dark aftermath of flames. . . .

Finally, he slept. His body was rigid, unmoving. His gray eyes opened. They did not open wide. They were slits cut into his face. They gleamed whitely in the darkness of the tent like the eyes of an animal.

He slept deeply, soundlessly, as though released from life.

He dreamed no dreams.

Fox Claw

Fox Claw rode alone through a driving rain. The night was wild and black around him, and that was good. He had no fear of being seen. He urged Watcher through the swollen waters of Cache Creek at Caddo Crossing. The high water, filled with mud but lighter than the night, roared around him.

The invisible fort of the *Taibos* was only a few hundred yards away, lost in the fury of the storm. The pounding sheets of rain washed away the *Taibo* smell, and that too was good. He turned south toward the reservation, his back to the fort.

He was tired. His ride had been long and hard. But he felt his spirit quickening as he approached the place of The People. He knew that his expectation was false, but he could not help himself. This was the way it had always been when The People had been free. It was different now, but a man could not easily change the feelings of a lifetime.

Ai-eee, how different it would have been then! How different it *had* been a few short years ago, in that other life.

Remember? How the men would paint themselves, what care they would take to look their very best! Before they came in from a raid they would rub the horses down with sweet grass, tie feathers in their manes and tails. The village would be waiting, alive with excitement. The women would chant the victory songs as they moved out to greet them. Ah, there would be dancing! Remember? How the drums would pound, the fire flames leap high into the air! The painted gleaming bodies would whirl and twist as every warrior acted out his exploits in pantomime. Faster and faster they would dance, they would go mad, they would dance until their blood pounded with the throbbing of the drums. And all the time the women would be watching, waiting. . . .

Ai-eee, it was all like a dream.

It was different now. Everything was different now.

They rode alone in the rain and darkness, he and Watcher. The war party had split up after burying their dead. Ten who had ridden with Fox Claw would ride no more. No, it was much worse than that. Would any man ever ride with him again? After losing ten warriors? After losing Sun Seeker?

They were slinking into camp as though they had been defeated, he and Watcher. They had not been beaten! They had charged the buffalo guns and they had won. They had brought back horses and mules.

He rode into the dripping cottonwoods, black sentinel shapes in the howling night. He was very close now.

He had fought and he had won. But there would be no welcome for him now. There would be no dance of victory. Ah, he knew them, he knew The People. They were not the same. They were afraid. They would cast anxious eyes toward the fort. They would not look at him.

The dogs came out at him, snapping at Watcher. He even had a different smell about him, he thought, different from the slow stink of the reservation. The dogs did not know him. He jabbed at their skinny rain-plastered bodies with the butt of his lance. They fell back, following him, splashing on padded feet through the gleaming mud.

He sensed the tepees around him. They rose like coned organic growths, pale against the black of the night. He could hear the rain drumming on the taut hide walls. Inside them, he knew, it would be warm—warm with the stale smoky air of sleep.

He took Watcher to a small clearing where the grass was good. He dismounted, his wet moccasins sinking into the soft earth. He lifted off the wooden saddle, peeled away the soaked buffalo robe. He removed the hair bridle. He stroked Watcher's streaming head and turned him loose. Watcher would not stray far.

He stepped through the mud, carrying his saddle and bridle, his buffalo robe, his rifle, and his lance. He staggered under their weight. He was clumsy and slow-footed away from his horse; he did not like to walk.

No one called to him. Every tepee was a sealed cone of silence.

He found his father's tepee more by memory than by sight. He dropped his saddle and bridle and buffalo robe. He took his lance in his right hand and drove it into the yielding earth outside the tepee. There were two fresh scalps on the lance. They were tiny things, hardly larger than the circle he could make with his thumb and forefinger. There had been no time to stretch them on the willow hoops. They danced jerkily in the pelting rain.

Carrying his rifle, he lifted the stiff pelt that covered

the teepee entrance. Dry yellow light spilled out into the darkness. He sniffed at the rich smells that puffed out at him. A remembered voice called out softly to him in greeting. His mother was awake.

Dripping wet, Fox Claw entered the tepee. The hard weighted hide fell back into place behind him, cutting off the night and the rain.

He moved toward the tiny fire.

His father stirred in the shadows, but did not speak.

Fox Claw slept late. The tepee was hot and stuffy before he roused himself. The rain had stopped and the tepee hides were damp and steaming. There was no one else in the tepee.

He got up, glad that he was alone. His father was old and sick. Words did not pass easily between them.

Fox Claw took his time, delaying his movement into the world outside. He dressed very carefully in clean dry clothing: his best beaded moccasins, the fringed buckskin leggings with the long broad flaps from the breechclout hanging over them almost to his knees, a soft V-necked deerskin shirt. He combed his straight black hair with his porcupine-tail brush, greased it, and tied it into two long braids with beaver fur. His hair was parted in a neat line down the middle, and he painted the part with a bold streak of vermilion. He fastened a single yellow feather in his scalp lock. He was ready, secure behind the shield of his clothing. It had taken him a little more than an hour to dress himself properly.

He pushed back the stiff hide cover and stepped out into the sunlight. He stood for a long moment, drinking in the sky. At first, he did not look at the people around him. The sun was warm on his shoulders. The wet earth had a good damp smell rising from it. Four jays squawked self-importantly in the branches of the cottonwood trees. He could hear the muted roar of the muddy water, still running high in the creek. The breeze that soothed his face was crisp and clean. Fox Claw was glad to be alive. Almost, he could forget where he was, and when he was.

But the old signs pressed in around him. They would not be ignored, those signs of defeat and despair. They thrust themselves upon him, choking off the freshness of the day.

Not twenty yards away from him he saw a bent old man leading a horse. He recognized Runs-Down-the-Antelope, recognized him despite his rags and the unkempt hair that hung down over his sunken eyes. (Runs-Down-the-Antelope! How proud he had once been, how full of spirit!) There was a bundle tied to the thin horse the old man led. It was not a large bundle. It contained the bones of the son of Runs-Down-the-Antelope. Three years and more it had been since his son had been killed, and still the old man kept the bones. Every night he took the bones into his tepee and placed them by the fire to warm.

Fox Claw thought of old Satank, the Kiowa. Satank was dead now, killed by MacKenzie's soldiers on his way to a Texas prison—Satank, even in chains, had tried to fight. Satank too had carried the bones of his son with him around the reservation. It had not been a good thing to see with Satank. It was not a good thing to see with Runs-Down-the-Antelope.

There were other signs, too many signs. He hated the men who wore the *Taibo* clothes—the baggy rumpled black suits with the dirty vests, the shoes that were as hard as stones, the dark stained hats that stuck up like hollow logs. Even the tepees mocked him. Slashed they were, scarred into ugly ribbons and squares where they had been patched with the white man's canvas. He watched the sickness around him, the sickness that had no name, the sickness that killed the eyes even while the body still seemed to live.

Fox Claw walked slowly away from his father's tepee. When the women saw him moving they began to wail. Ten men who had ridden away with him had not returned. There was an emptiness in many tepees.

Fox Claw refused to hurry his steps. He held his head high, looking straight before him. Let the women cry, let them smear their faces with black paint, let them strike the tepees of the slain! He was no woman. He was a Comanche warrior.

Let them fill their eyes. Let them look at a man. Fox

Claw was vain enough to wish for his horse; he looked better on Watcher. It was hard to be proud while walking.

He was tall for a Comanche, tall and skinny and tough. His movements lacked grace; he walked jerkily, a stiff-jointed skeleton all dressed and painted and intruding on the masquerade of life. His thin face was sharp and direct; there was nothing subtle about it. There were gaunt hollows under his jutting cheekbones. His face had a rough, unfinished look about it—almost a careless look. It might have been hacked out of granite by an indifferent medicine hammer. His eyes were his best feature. Hard and black they were, and fever-bright. They were steady eyes, deep spring-water eyes, cold and clear and still.

How different everything was, and how strange! There were no good food smells in the air. The children seemed deformed with their bloated bellies and stick-thin arms and legs. There was no joy in the village, and no hope. The sickness fouled the air.

He walked on, his back straight. He glanced at the tepee of Warm Wind, but he did not see her. Tonight, he would have a tepee of his own. He was too old to stay with his father. The women of his family were putting it up now in the shade of the cottonwoods. Tonight, he would have a place for Warm Wind. She would come or she would not come. He could not command her.

He pushed his thoughts away from him. There was a day to endure, a day with nothing in it, a hollow day. He had spent many such days on the reservation, too many. He had learned the way. He moved toward the old tepee of Dies Young. Dies Young had not changed, would never change. He would have whiskey. That was one of the two good things that the *Taibos* had brought. The other was the rifle.

Whiskey was what he needed now.

That was all there was, in this place, in this time.

The shadows lengthened and the evening winds stirred across the purpled land. The oaks and pecans that lined the muddy stream whispered in their dark branches. The doves called softly to each other. Fox Claw sat silently before his tepee and watched the death of the day.

He waited for what had to come. It took a long time. The sun was buried and the first stars were clear in the night sky before he heard the flat thudding boom that echoed thinly across the reservation. The sunset gun at Sill. He took it as a personal insult; the whiskey was strong in him.

Had not the treaty of Medicine Lodge given this land to The People and to their Kiowa friends? Yes, and had not the soldiers come and built the fort only three years later? And did not the madmen, the Quakers, speak to them of peace whenever they handed out the tasteless food? Yes, and had the treaty stopped the hunters from slaughtering the buffalo on the old Comanche hunting grounds?

There could be no life without the buffalo! Even a child knew this. The buffalos were meat and clothing and shelter and fuel, but they were still more. The buffalo and the Comanche were one. As well take away his horse as his buffalo! Let the Indians of the Pueblos grow corn and beans if they wished. Let the Apaches do it and the Mexicans and the Texans. A Comanche man did not grub in the dirt like a woman scratching for roots. The Comanches were hunters. The Comanches were fighters. A man could not feed his body on plants!

Disgusted, he went into his tepee. He built a small fire in the round hole the women had dug, kindling it with Mexican flint and steel. The smoke drifted up and out through the smokehole just below the top of the tepee. He moved to the back of his lodge and sat cross-legged on the buffalo robe that covered his slightly raised bed.

If Warm Wind were coming, she would not come until late. It would not be proper. His lip curled. Warm Wind would not wish to be seen with him. She had refused his horses twice. She wanted to be the woman of Cripple Colt. Warm Wind was thinking the new way, the reservation way. Cripple Colt was tame and safe. He would live for a long time.

Still, she would come to him. She had always come.

He was not drunk, through no fault of his own. Dies Young had had very little whiskey, and that had been mostly water and gunpowder. It had been enough to ease the emptiness in his belly. It had been enough to make him a little sorry for himself.

He sat very still. The village was quiet now except for the occasional barking of the dogs. He was hungry, but it did not even occur to him that he might kill a dog and eat it. He had not had a dog of his own for many years, but that did not matter. Was not the dog the cousin of Coyote?

This should have been the night of the scalp dance. The village should be alive with fires and drums. It hurt him to be alone on this night.

Then Warm Wind came. She stood there shyly, just inside the tepee, not looking directly at him. She had dressed with care, and this pleased him. The beads on her long deerskin dress glittered in the soft light of the tiny fire. Bracelets gleamed on her wrists. Her dark eyes were outlined in yellow and she had a solid triangle of red painted on each cheek.

"Sit," said Fox Claw.

She knelt on the other side of the fire, away from him. She did not speak. Her close-cropped hair framed a face that was good to see in the gentle light; the strong line of her jaw was softened and the hunger-lines were smoothed.

"I am glad that you have come." Fox Claw stood up but made no move toward her. There was a tension between them; it was as though their bodies had never joined. He felt uncertain, like a boy.

Warm Wind said nothing, but she looked at him openly now. Her eyes shone. She seemed ageless and yet somehow very young. He could remember her as a girl, playing with a toy bull-roarer. She would swing the flat cedar board through the summer air, holding it by the thong tied to the handle, listening with a child's delight to the whirring noise it made. Her eyes had been very bright then, as they were now. That was the way she had received her name; the *yuane*, the bull-roarer, was named after the sound of warm wind it made when it was buzzed through the air.

"Tonight—there should have been the victory dance," Fox Claw said abruptly. It seemed a very important, urgent thing to say.

"Tell me," Warm Wind said. "I will listen."

Fox Claw knew an instant of shame, shame that he felt the need of boasting to a woman. But he could not help himself. He felt suddenly released. There was a kind of madness flowing within him, a good madness, a madness in which a man might lose himself.

It was hot in the tepee. He pulled off his shirt and leggings. When he moved, the long muscles in his thin arms and legs twisted like ropes. His neck was unusually thick and strong, too big to support the craggy skull of his face; his neck swelled in the firelight like a puffing snake.

"You saw the scalps on my lance, the scalps of the *Taibos*."

"I saw them."

Fox Claw crouched slightly. His voice grew louder. "I counted coup. Twice I counted coup. Fox Claw is a warrior. All of The People know that Fox Claw is a warrior!"

The words were a formula, but they were strong. They seized him, transported him. This, at last, was right. This was how it was meant to be.

The tiny fire seemed to grow until it filled the tepee. His blood pounded with a drumlike rhythm. He lost himself, surrendered to his spirit. Ai-eee, he was strong medicine! His body jerked and lunged in the confined space of the tepee, acting out the raid. Sweat beaded his dark skin. His eyes were wild; his eyes were the wind and the night and the sweep of the plains, his eyes were the fury of battle.

Warm Wind watched and listened.

Finally, his voice trailed away. His body slackened. He sank down on the bed, exhausted. Ah, where were the drums? What had happened to the great fire? Where were the shouts of The People?

There was only a terrible silence.

He closed his eyes. He was alone, alone! He had been a fool, prancing and shouting for a woman. He was not a warrior. There were no warriors, not any more.

His body twisted convulsively on the bed. He hated himself. Hated his weakness.

Blindly, he reached out for Warm Wind. She was

there, she was there. He clutched her until she whimpered with pain. He must not let her go. She must stay with him!

He heard her voice. "I will stay. I will stay."

He did not wait, could not wait. He took her body, took it with a violence that was more anger than love, more despair than need. When it was over, they were both weak and trembling. It passed; their bodies stilled. Fox Claw felt a warm, comfortable drowsiness. He did not feel love, or even tenderness. Dimly, sleepily, he was grateful to Warm Wind—but only a little. This was his right. This was the way things should be. That was all.

"Sleep now," she said, her breath fevered in his ear. "I will stay."

Fox Claw slept.

His dreams were good.

They were awake long before the dawn. Warm Wind had to be back in her own tepee before it was light. It was not proper to be bold. It would mark her forever.

Warm Wind loved him, perhaps. But love was not everything; it was not enough. She was a woman, with a woman's ancient wisdom. She wanted a life for herself and for her children in this strange new world in which she found herself. Fox Claw was a bad gamble. He had the old wildness in him. Her father and her brothers had other plans for Warm Wind. It was her father who had twice refused the horses of Fox Claw. Warm Wind was only a woman. She could not easily go against the wishes of her family. And Warm Wind was not eager to throw her life away.

Fox Claw understood these things. He had a contempt for Cripple Colt. In the old days, Cripple Colt would have been nothing and less than nothing. He would have been a woman himself. But he felt no contempt for Warm Wind. It was different for a woman.

They came together again, slowly, without fury. There was still plenty of time. It was like a greeting, a comfortable greeting, and that was the significance they both gave to it. Then Warm Wind roused herself and built up the fire; Fox Claw would not even think of doing it himself while there was a woman in his tepee.

They could talk now. They were natural with each other.

"Has it been a hard time for you?" he asked.

"There has been little food," she said slowly. It was not good for a woman to complain. "There has been much sickness."

He shook his head. "It is a shameful time. It is wrong for us to stay here to be herded like the *Taibo* cattle."

"There is nowhere else to go."

He touched her. "There are the Staked Plains. The soldiers do not know the Staked Plains. The buffalo are still there. The Kwahadis are still there. They are free."

"For how long?" She looked up at him, her yellow-rimmed eyes filled with words that could not be spoken. "The old days are gone."

"The old days! What of the old days? There has always been fighting. Did we not take this land from the Apaches? Did we not fight the Tonkawas and the Pawnees? Did we not fight the Mexicans? We can fight the soldiers too."

"Perhaps. It is not for me to say."

"Have you heard nothing? Am I the only warrior left?"

"I have heard some talk. Yes. I do not know what it means."

"What talk have you heard?"

"There is a man. Do you remember Ishatai?"

"The son of the medicine man? Yes, I remember him. He is no warrior."

"It is said that he has great power."

"Ah. I have heard such things before. It is not his kind of power that we need."

"I do not know. But Ishatai has done strange things. He foretold a great light in the sky, and it happened as he said. I myself saw it. They say that he has brought back some of the dead. They say he has traveled above the clouds and spoken to the great spirits. They say that he has dreamed great medicine dreams."

"Others have dreamed, but we are here. Ishatai is young."

"It is hard to know about these things. But Ishatai says that he has the power. He speaks of it openly to all who will listen. I have seen him with my own eyes spit up bullets from his belly. It is said that the *Taibos* cannot harm him. It is said by some that he can lead the people back. It is said that he will dream more dreams, and the dreams will have power."

"You saw him do this thing with the bullets?"

"I saw him."

"That is strong medicine."

"I am only a woman. I do not know what to believe."

"I will speak with Ishatai. It may be that his words are good."

"It may be." Warm Wind looked toward the entrance to the tepee. There was light there from the rising sun. "It is time."

"Yes. It is time."

They spoke no more. She rose from the bed, dressed, and slipped out through the door hole. She left an emptiness behind her. It had been good not to be alone.

He waited until the sky grew lighter. Then he pulled on his leggings and his shirt and stepped outside into the cold. He stood before his tepee, his thin arms folded across his chest.

The eastern sky was painted with yellow and purple and rose; the clouds were alive. The air was very still. The camp was silent around him. He watched the red sun burn its way out of the earth and begin its long journey across the sky. Somehow, he was reassured. This, at least, had not changed.

He breathed deeply, filling his lungs with the sweet cold air.

Far, far away—it seemed to come from another world—he heard the faint clear call of the morning bugle from the fort.

There was a pulse of hope in his heart, a pulse of life. It could be, it might be. Even if the words of Ishatai were false, he might use them. They were something.

He would listen when Ishatai spoke. He would see.

Speak soon, O Ishatai!
The days are long, but the days are few.
Soon there will be no more days, no more suns.
Soon The People will be no more.
Speak soon, O Ishatai!
And speak well, speak well!

Curtis

Curtis stood on the wooden steps of his headquarters office building at Fort Wade, his thumbs hooked in his waist belt. Ostensibly, he was waiting for Matt to come in with Trooper King from D Company. Actually, however, this was no more than an excuse to get out of his office. He didn't give a damn about Trooper King, for the good and simple reason that he didn't have to give a damn about him.

Trooper King was a snowbird. He had enlisted in the army to get a handout all winter, and at the first sign of spring he had gone over the hill. Curtis could understand the logic, but he had no intention of letting King get away with it. An army without discipline was no army at all. There were those—some of them in very high places—who winked at this sort of desertion. "Let them go," they said, lighting up their big cigars. "They build up the West." Fortunately or otherwise, those men did not have to lead troops into battle. Curtis had no inclination whatever to lead an unreliable rabble against the Indians. But Matt Irvine could handle Trooper King without any help from Curtis. Matt would probably shoot him and have a good time doing it.

Curtis stared blankly at the three kids who were tied to the flagpole in the center of the parade ground. The sight was too familiar to register. Mothers at the fort often hooked their toddlers on a line fastened to the flagpole to keep them out of mischief. The ground was still muddy, and the children were having a fine time.

He stood there on the steps where he had stood so many times before. His hands were clammy, but that was the only sign of the tension that was in him. Outwardly, he seemed confident and relaxed. The weak cloud-shadowed sun picked out flecks of silver in his long, fine brown hair. He looked distinguished; he knew it, and it amused him and pleased him at the same time. He looked as though he were about to sit for an oil portrait: Frontier Cavalry Officer, perhaps, or Hero of the Indian Wars. He was forty-seven years old and they had not been easy years, but he was a man who carried his age gracefully. He was six feet four and weighed one hundred and eighty pounds. Oddly, it was not his height that struck an observer, or even the slim trimness of his uniformed body. It was his face that dominated his appearance, and his eyes dominated his face. His eyes were a very light gray, so light that they seemed unnatural. People said that his eyes were cold, an impression that was helped by his thin, close-lipped smile. Actually, his smile was what it was because his teeth were bad, and his eyes, despite their directness and depth, could be warm enough on occasion. His nose was strong and prominent, his brown eyebrows were heavy. His face was long and narrow, furrowed with hard lines. It was not a face that encouraged easy intimacy, but it was the face of a man a soldier could follow with confidence.

Fort Wade was as much of a home as he had ever had as a man. He had built Fort Wade. He had been its only C.O. It was nothing fancy, but he had no taste for fancy things. A well-worn parade ground, flanked by the usual drab plank buildings: Officers' Row opposite the barnlike barracks for the men, the headquarters offices on the south side of the square, the proverbially inadequate hospital, the quartermaster and ordnance storehouses, the shops, the guardhouse with its barred windows. All were painted a uniformly dismal color that had once been gray. And there was a Sudsville, of course, for the married soldiers. And the sutler's store, which doubled as an officers' club and canteen. A wooden palisade surrounded the fort, and a second palisade, to the east, took care of the stables and the hay yard. It wasn't much, but it was four years of his life.

The mission of Fort Wade was simple enough in theory if not in practice. (That, Curtis reflected, was a capsule history of the affairs of mankind.) Fort Wade's job, and the task of the units of the Twelfth Cavalry stationed there, was to protect the people of Texas from Indian raids and to engage any hostile Indians caught off the reservation. It sounded easy. There were only a few small problems. How, for example, did you catch the wind? How did you defend against phantoms? How could you strike a telling blow against an enemy that could always retreat to a legally invincible fortress, a fortress thoughtfully provided by the same United States Government that ordered you to engage the hostile Indians? And if you could not strike a decisive, effective blow, how could you protect the people of Texas? All the Indians had to do was to sneak off the reservation, make a fast raid, and sneak back to the reservation again.

Curtis took a deep breath. He had stalled long enough; there was no point in waiting any longer for Trooper King. He still had to prepare his report. What was worse, he would have to write the thing himself. His adjutant was once again engaged in the Great Battle of the Pears. The Great Battle had started when the post surgeon had rashly condemned a can of pears from the commissary. The department quartermaster had reacted by sending the offending can of pears to Washington, requesting a fast analysis by government chemists. The chemists replied that the pears were in fine shape. Darkly, the quartermaster threatened to take action against the post surgeon. The doctor got *his* feathers ruffled and stalked about fulminating against the inhuman quartermaster. There had been twenty-two official letters so far, and the end was nowhere in sight.

Oh, the drums would roll. Upon my soul, this is the style we'd go:
"Forty miles a day on beans and hay in the Regular Army O!"

It was a great life.

Curtis walked into his office and sat down at his desk. He began his report. He was tempted to head the report with the most appropriate name for the post: Fort Wait, Texas. He stifled the impulse, as always. With quick, precise strokes of his goose quill pen he wrote a clear and orderly account of the death of the buffalo hunters. He mentioned the tracks he had seen, and spelled out what seemed to him to be the implications of the fight. The Indians were taking long chances, and they were willing to lose men in an attack on a fairly well defended position. That meant that more trouble was certainly ahead.

There were some things that he could not put in a report, but he was confident that Sheridan was no fool. He could read between the lines.

One of the most difficult things about this campaign was the fact that it was next to impossible for Curtis to anticipate the exact moves of his enemy. He could not know when they would strike, or where, or in what force. In the War, it had been different. A man had at least some notion of the generals who were opposing him, and he knew roughly what forces those generals had available. But who led the Comanches? There was no chief of the Comanche tribe, there were no Comanche generals under any name. Any young buck with a thirst for glory—and that meant all young bucks, or nearly all of them—could lead a raid whenever the urge hit him; all he had to do was to round up some warriors who would accept his leadership for the duration of the raid. Or perhaps there was no glory question involved; he might just want some horses, or he might have a grudge, or he might have had a big dream. There might be a plan for a raid, but there was no overall strategy for the tribe. A raid could involve only five or six men, or it could include several hundred, depending on the prestige of the raid leader. To make matters worse, nobody really knew how many Comanches there were. The Comanches themselves didn't know, and Curtis certainly didn't. There might have been two or three thousand warriors in the tribe, but they never fought together as a massed unit. They weren't even all together in one place—there were probably more Comanches off the reservation than on it at any given time. And then there were the Kiowas. They were a different breed of cat, but they had been tied in with the Comanches for a long time. And if the Cheyennes moved south. . . .

Curtis fired up his pipe. It was futile to stew about the Kiowas, idiotic to speculate about the Cheyennes. The Comanches were his major problem. They were a tough nut to crack, but he knew that he could beat them. He knew how to do it; what he lacked was the *authority* to do it. No matter how he cut the cards, he always wound up with the same hand. There was nothing he could do except to make the same two recommendations he had made before, so he proceeded to make them.

First, the army had to remove its weight from its collective saddle sores and take the offensive against the Indians. The cavalry was an offensive weapon; the only sane way to employ it was to have it take the offensive. It was wasteful folly to chase isolated parties of raiders back and forth across the plains. Usually, he could not catch them. If he did catch them, his victory could not be decisive. The army should move in force against the hostiles in the Staked Plains, where most of them were hiding. The army should hunt them down, attack their camps, wipe them out if necessary.

Second, the Fort Sill reservation had to be drastically reorganized. It was all very well to give the Indians a place where they could live in peace, give them an alternative to fighting. Curtis did not question that. But it was crazy to permit the reservation to be used as a sanctuary for hostile raiders. The Indians on the reservation should be disarmed, dismounted, and counted at regular intervals. It would be simple enough to detect the lawbreakers. Once the guilty ones were caught, they should be sent to prison and kept there until they got some sense.

Simple? Certainly. Curtis did not flatter himself that his plan was brilliant. It was little more than common sense. He wondered how many lives it would take before his two elementary suggestions became orders.

He signed his report and was surprised to notice how late it had become. It was getting hard to see in his office without a light. He pushed back his chair and got to his feet. His right leg was bothering him again; the knee, which was stiff from a chunk of metal he had run into at Antietam, had been rubbing against the desk. He smiled sourly. That, he thought, was his visible wound from the War. The real scars went deeper, and a man got no medals for them. He straightened his uniform and clamped on his new hat. He was fond of the hat, which had its brim pulled up in front and fastened with the crossed sabers of the cavalry. It wasn't strictly regulation, but then rank still had some privileges.

He hurried out to the parade ground. The long sunset shadows striped the waiting blue-clad troops; he was just in time. He stood at attention as the flag was lowered, enjoying the clean, pure notes of the bugles. He took the salute of the marching men with genuine pride and satisfaction. By God, they *looked* like soldiers. He thought that the men of D Company seemed a trifle shamefaced about the absent Trooper King, but that may have been only his imagination. (There were some who were beginning to call cavalry units troops rather than companies, but Curtis was in no hurry to change.) The guard detail marched off with Captain Taylor of C Company, who was officer of the day, and the men were dismissed. Yellow lights were already gleaming in the mess hall.

Curtis remembered that he was hungry, which was not something that he often forgot. He had been hungry a lot lately. He and Helen had brought in an Eastern girl to do the cooking for them. Being experienced in such matters, they had hired the homeliest girl they could find; she had been a walking insult to her sex. It hadn't done any good at all. She had been married off within three weeks of her arrival at Wade. Damn sergeants anyhow! If Helen served more of that eggless custard tonight—

He sighed and walked across the shadowed parade ground to his house. He did not want to go there. His nerves were on edge. He needed Maria, needed her with an urgency that was almost a sickness. But that was impossible.

He went home, to Helen.

* * *

After supper—which had, as he had feared, been anticlimaxed with more of the deadly cornstarch custard—Curtis sought refuge in his big stuffed armchair in the parlor. It was a comfortable room; Helen had done wonders with it. There were bright curtains on the windows and cheerful prints of sunsets and Greek nymphs on the walls. Curtis tried to bury himself in the new *Cavalry Journal*, with very indifferent success.

Helen sat on the couch across from him, her sewing basket by her side. She sat very primly; she was every inch the colonel's lady, even in the privacy of their own parlor. Her long cotton dress was stiff with starch. Her soft brown hair, pulled back into a bun, was neat and orderly. Only her clear blue eyes seemed alive. She talked incessantly. She said that she wanted to take up the guitar again, and that Mary Irvine was willing to teach her. She said that she was making a dress from a new Butterick pattern. She said that the dogs on the post kept her awake at night with their barking.

Curtis tried to make some appropriate responses. He knew that Helen's chatter was an attempt to reach out to him, make contact with him. He felt guilty at his own lack of interest. Helen was still an attractive woman, but he had never been able to talk to her about anything that mattered.

He pretended to go on reading. With each passing year the gap between them widened. He was fond of Helen, but that was the way it was. It was certainly not her fault that she had married the wrong man. In a way, he sometimes thought, Helen had not married any particular man—she had married the army. He had courted her on an army post, they had walked under the arch of crossed sabers together, and they had always lived with the army around them—and between them. In the days when he had still tried to joke with her, he had once said that the only reason she had married him was that he was distantly related to General Miles, whose mother had been a Curtis. She was still thrilled when the men rode out to the strains of "The Girl I Left Behind Me." By all the conventional tokens, she had been a good wife to him—a good, dutiful wife to a romantic cavalry officer. But she did not know Curtis. She had never known him.

It was not just sex, although that was a part of it. Helen had never been a passionate woman; there had been no spark in her, even in the early days of their marriage. And something had died in her with the death of their only child, a son, too many years before. Helen seldom refused him, but Curtis could not lose himself in her. There was still something virginal about her lovemaking, something reserved and unyielding and afraid.

Of course, he knew, it was not all Helen's fault. He was not an ideal husband. It may have been that he did not know his wife any more than she knew him.

She worried about him, yes. She knew that when he rode out with the band playing he might not come back. It had been just before Christmas when Lieutenant Godfrey had taken a Comanche arrow in the throat. Mrs. Godfrey had gone into her house, sat down in a chair, placed the muzzle of her husband's Colt .44 carefully in her mouth, and pulled the trigger. Helen might have done the same if Curtis had failed to come back. She loved him, as she understood love. For some men, that would have been enough. It wasn't enough for Curtis.

He tossed aside the magazine. He did not look at his wife. He could not read, not tonight, and he had been a reading man all his life. He remembered the astonishment of the correspondent he had met two years ago at Sill, where he had gone to meet Maria. That young man, with the smug sureness of people who had never been there, people who invented their own myths and then actually believed in them, was absolutely convinced that everyone on the frontier was an ignorant lout. He had flatly refused to believe that Major Forsyth had been reading *Oliver Twist* when he had been rescued after the bloody battle of Beecher's Island—and that with three bullet wounds in him from the Cheyenne and the Sioux. He had smiled politely when Curtis had told him about an officer he knew who spent his evenings between fights in translating the odes of Horace.

Curtis wanted to read. He wanted to forget himself in a book, a good fat book like *Moby Dick*. Or perhaps

Emerson. He had heard Emerson speak many times in Massachusetts. If he could find the right essay—

It was no use. Helen was at him about the dogs again.

Curtis stood up. "I'll go out and do what I can. Go on to bed, don't wait up for me. I may take a walk around."

She looked at him, her eyes troubled. "You won't be late?"

"Go on to bed, Helen. I'll be along later."

"You need your rest." She had sent him away and now she was reluctant to let him go. She sensed that she had failed him in some way, but she did not know how or why. She did not want to be alone, and she did not want him to be alone.

"Go to bed, Helen." His voice was sharper than he had intended.

He did not make it worse by saying more. He left the house, moving quickly. The cool night air touched his face. He welcomed the darkness, the isolation. He clenched his fists. His palms were wet with sweat.

The dogs of Fort Wade found him and welcomed him. His night walks after taps had given him a familiar smell to the hounds. They knew him. There were five of them out tonight, three of them belonging to Matt. They wagged their burr-clogged tails and jumped up on him. He took them one at a time, whispering to them, scratching their ears, calming them down.

Curtis had no intention of trying to enforce the standing order about the dogs. Ever since Wade had been built, that order had gone out faithfully twice a year, instructing owners to keep their dogs tied at night. The orders had been universally ignored. Curtis didn't like to see dogs tied.

He walked on, the hounds pacing happily and quietly around him. No one challenged him in the silent fort. The night watch saw him, of course, but they were used to his walks. There were drawbacks to being a commanding officer. It was impossible for him to get off by himself without being seen. There was no place near Fort Wade where he could bring Maria without setting the barracks buzzing. No matter how much he needed Maria, he would not subject Helen to that kind of talk.

And he did need Maria. He needed her tonight.

"The hell with it," he said softly.

The Indians would be out tonight, somewhere. They too would be drinking in the cold night air under the star-sparked immensity of the sky. They would be dreaming their dreams, making their plans. Well, he could handle them if it came to a fight. The Indians could be dangerous, could be brave to the point of insanity. But they had no discipline, no control. Their tactics were few and easily anticipated. As far as Curtis was concerned, any officer who got himself caught in an Indian trap was a thundering fool. He could beat them. But sometimes, in the night, he felt very close to them. He wished that he too could be beyond the fort, riding the dark land, free with the wind and the stars. . . .

He took a deep breath. He said good night to the dogs and walked back to the house and went inside. Helen had left the lamp burning by his chair.

He got a bottle of whiskey and a glass and sat down. He did not want to get drunk. He knew exactly how much he needed. There was something wild in him, something dark and buried, something that he had to control. The whiskey helped, sometimes. He drank slowly but steadily until the edge was off. Then he replaced the bottle, turned down the lamp, and blew it out.

He undressed in the dark.

He went to Helen's bed.

He took her gently, without passion. She murmured in his ear but he could not tell whether she was fully awake or not.

Curtis went back to his own bed. He went to sleep quickly, deeply. His gray eyes opened to slits and gleamed in the night, staring at nothing.

In the bed next to his, Helen stirred and sat up. She looked across at the shadowed form of her husband. Satisfied that he was there, she burrowed into the covers and went back to sleep.

Fox Claw

It had been a long afternoon, long and empty and gray, one of a dispirited procession of slow days that trudged by in single file, going nowhere. There was no breath of promise in the April air, no stirrings of life, no awakening.

Ishatai had not spoken.

Fox Claw was hungry. His belly was a tight knot twisted under his skin. His hunger was not sharp, not demanding—it was simply there, a part of him forever. He had no false memories about the taste of spring buffalo meat, but the tongues were always good. He had asked the *kusetemini*, the horned toad, about the buffalo. The horned toad had scrabbled away in the general direction of the Staked Plains. There would be buffalo there; the *kusetemini* would not lie. Fox Claw hated the reservation food, what there was of it. No man could eat salt pork and live.

If Ishatai did not speak soon—

He brought his attention back to the words of Buffalo Tongue. The boy with the name that reminded him of good food had been telling him of his buffalo hunt for hours. The boy looked up to Fox Claw, depended on him. He had to listen.

"I have killed the buffalo," the boy said. "With my lance I have killed the buffalo, though I am not yet a man, a warrior like you. I have taken the first step. But my path is blocked before me. How can I walk the path when there is no path?"

"You are young, *tua*. There is time for you."

"The time is now! Take me with you when you go."

"Your father would not be pleased, *tua*."

"But you are also my father."

"Yes." Fox Claw looked at the boy. Ai-eee, well he

knew the hungers that raged through the blood of a boy! The hunger for food—that was nothing, that came later. But the hunger to be a man, to go on the warpath, to be brave in the eyes of the girls—that was the hunger of youth, the desire that could not be patient. He remembered, he remembered. "I am proud to call you my son, my *tua*. Your father is my brother and you are my son. But you must have the medicine before you can ride with me. It is the way."

Buffalo Tongue looked at the ground, shamed. "I have tried, my father. I climbed Medicine Bluff alone. I carried my bone pipe and my tobacco. Four days and four nights I waited. Yet I saw nothing. There was no medicine."

"It is not enough to try." Fox Claw groped for words. "The Wichita Mountains have lost much power. There are too many *Taibos* here. The *Taibos* are not good for dreams."

"Where can I go?"

Fox Claw smiled a little. It was pleasant to be with a boy who thought that he, Fox Claw, knew the answers to the ancient questions. Answers? There were no answers, not any more. But he could not tell that to a boy. "There are many places. One day, perhaps, I will take you."

"When?"

"When the time is right, *tua*. The world has changed. If you would be a man, you must learn to wait."

"Waiting is hard. I am not yet a man."

"Waiting is always hard, even for a man."

Buffalo Tongue stood up, restlessly.

Speak, Ishatai!

"Go see to the horses, *tua*," Fox Claw said gently.

Buffalo Tongue walked away, his head held high. Fox Claw sat alone, staring at nothing.

Soon, he got up and went to find Dies Young.

Dies Young, as usual, was feeling no pain.

Fox Claw had great admiration for his friend's uncanny ability to convert horses into whiskey and whiskey into horses in an endless magical cycle. Whatever Dies Young felt, whatever dark thoughts he lived with, he had not lost his style. Now he was getting drunk again, and he was doing it properly.

Naked except for his breechclout and moccasins, he sat cross-legged in his tepee, clutching his bottle of terrible whiskey like a war club. He looked like a painted spider in the uncertain light, a bloated spider that had somehow, improbably, sprouted a single drooping black feather. Dies Young had a massive head; it was like a weathered chunk of sandstone framed by the darker obsidian of his hair. His eyes were little more than slits in the heavy flesh of his face. His short, stocky body was too squat and powerful to be graceful, and his arms and legs seemed too skinny for him. Without his horse, Dies Young was nothing much to look at. A stranger might even have called him ugly. But you had to see Dies Young on his horse to know him. Dies Young was the best horseman Fox Claw had ever known, and Fox Claw had known the best there were. His horse transformed Dies Young, even more than most Comanches. Mounted, he was beautiful; there was no other word for him. In a fight he was worth five men. Dies Young had not acquired his name through an excess of timidity.

"Drink!" he grunted, thrusting out the bottle. "It builds a fire in your belly."

Fox Claw accepted the bottle. He took a good swallow and gasped. The whiskey hit his empty stomach and bounced dangerously, but he kept it down. Whiskey was too precious to waste.

"Ah," said Dies Young. "It is good. Drink more. I have been thinking good thoughts."

Fox Claw took another pull at the bottle. He sat down, rather more rapidly than he had intended. Whiskey was better at a feast, when the belly was full. But there were no feasts now. There was only the whiskey. "My friend has been thinking?"

Dies Young laughed—a great deep gurgle of a laugh. "Good thoughts! Ai-eee, it is we who have been children, you and I. We have been fools. Fools to ride so far, my friend. I have truly been thinking. A great thought has been given to me. Do we not have enemies close at hand? Do not these enemies have horses?"

Fox Claw frowned. Surely, Dies Young wasn't *that* drunk. "Not the soldiers?"

"The soldiers! Yes, yes, the soldiers. They have many horses, good horses. I can almost smell them! A man could *walk* to them."

"Your thoughts are dangerous, my friend. How could we attack the fort where the soldiers live?"

"Drink," Dies Young whispered. "It clears the head." He raised his voice again. "Are we women? Are we corn-growers, scratchers in the dirt? I can steal horses *anywhere*."

Fox Claw took another drink, a small one. His friend's idea still seemed stupid. "There are too many soldiers."

"Think, my friend! Who speaks of the fort? Not I. Who speaks of blue soldiers who cover the earth like clouds of grasshoppers? Not I. *I* speak only of horses. Think! Where are the horses and who is guarding them?"

Fox Claw still did not understand. He knew where the horses were, of course. Once he saw horses he did not forget them. "There are stables on the west side of the fort. They are behind the barracks. We could not get to them."

Dies Young grinned. "And are those the only horses?"

"No." Fox Claw felt his heart begin to thud in his chest. "There is the other place. They call it the quartermaster corral. It is to the east of the fort, on the flats of Cache Creek. It too has horses and mules. I have seen them."

"Yes, and at night who watches those horses and mules?"

"The animals are hobbled, that I know. I have heard it said that there are only two sentries there at night. . . ."

"Two soldiers! They are nothing. They might as well *give* us the horses. Do you know how many horses and mules they keep there?"

"No. I do not know."

"*I* know. I have counted them. There are seventy-three horses and mules kept in that corral at night. This was true last night. This will be true on this night. Two soldiers for seventy-three horses and mules!"

Fox Claw answered the smile of Dies Young. "It is as

you said. You have been thinking." He was not yet ready to commit himself, however. There was no hurry. After all, one bottle was small enough preparation for truly *great* thoughts. "Remember. There will be other soldiers."

"I do not fear them. Let them come."

"Our talk is big. It is good talk. But we cannot fight the entire army, you and I."

Dies Young reared himself to his full height, a buffalo on the legs of an antelope. "I have a plan. Yes. I myself will take care of the soldiers from the fort when they come. *You* will take the horses and mules and ride for the Staked Plains. I will join you there when I have exhausted the horses of the soldiers. Do you think I cannot do what I say?"

"If you say you will do it, you will do it."

"Ah, think of it, my friend! To sneak through the very body-stink of the *Taibos* and run off with their horses. A coup to remember, a coup to tell of around many fires."

Fox Claw still hesitated. "We will need others. I cannot herd so many horses and mules alone—not even if you are prepared to fight the army by yourself."

"You are growing old, my friend. You worry too much."

"I have not changed." Fox Claw spoke more loudly than he had intended.

"You will need others, that is true. Well, there will be others. Not everyone here is dead. White Horse of the Kiowas will go. Tenebeka will go. Black Bear will ride with us. Perhaps some of the younger men . . . ."

"You know that I have been talking with Buffalo Tongue?"

"I know." Dies Young always knew.

"He does not yet have his medicine."

"We have enough medicine for all, you and I. We will take care of Buffalo Tongue."

"There are some who must not know of this thing. Cripple Colt—he talks too much to Reed. And Kicking Bird—he also talks too much with the agent."

"Kicking Bird! Do not speak of fools. Ah, listen!"

A rumble of thunder sounded in the east, heavy and

threatening. A faint cool breeze stirred through the open tepee entrance.

"It is a sign." Dies Young whispered. "Tonight will be a good night. It will be dark and filled with rain. They will never even see us. It will be too easy!"

"Let us finish the whiskey," said Fox Claw.

There wasn't much left in the bottle, but they made good use of it. To Fox Claw, the plan of his friend now seemed completely logical. It might be that in time Ishatai would speak of his dreams, and that was well. But there was still work that men could do.

Work, yes—but more than work. It was a kind of game they were about to play, an ancient and deadly game, a game that warmed the head and the heart and the blood. They had to have horses, yes. The People had been nothing before the horses had come, and a man was a man only to the extent that he could get more horses. They had to strike a blow against the soldiers, yes; they could not sit like women on the reservation and call themselves Comanches. There were old scores to settle, there was honor to renew. But the game was important for itself. The game was fun, the game was excitement, the game was the measure of a man. It was a joke, a great joke to play on the *Taibos*. And it was defiance, phrased in the only language they knew.

If the time came when the game was no longer played, The People would be—changed. They would not be The People.

They went out into the village, seeking their friends. They were men and they were boys again. They were warriors and pranksters, proud and foolish, cunning and carefree. Laughter had come into their hearts again.

The welcome sound of thunder muttered in the afternoon shadows.

Dies Young had been right. It would be a good time. Dark and full of rain. . . .

The two Tenth Cavalry troopers who had drawn the guard detail at the quartermaster corral were not thinking about Indians. In general, they were thinking about the miserably wet spring of 1874. In particular, they were thinking about how to make small targets of themselves in the torrential rain that poured down out of the black April night. The gray limestone barracks of Fort Sill seemed very far away.

The horses and mules inside the stake-and-rider rail corral were nervous and restless in the storm. In the jagged white flashes of lightning that ripped the darkness the hides of the animals gleamed and glistened with liquid flame. The thunder boomed like hell's own artillery, and the earth was a sea of muddy water.

The troopers, both of whom had been plantation hands in Arkansas not too many years before, were not expecting any trouble. They had drawn a dirty duty and they were looking for an excuse, any excuse, to get out of the downpour. Shortly after midnight, they got all the excuse that any reasonable man could require.

A livid fork of lightning, the kind that makes the heart skip a beat, transformed the wild night into instant day. Before the blackness closed in again, in the eerie light that almost blinded the eyes, the soldiers saw two things with sudden, abysmal clarity. There was a painted naked Indian inside the corral snapping a wet blanket at the rearing animals; the bars of the corral were already down. And there was a mounted Comanche, riding like a demon, coming straight at them. He rode like a madman, hanging miraculously on the left side of his rain-slick mustang, and he had a very long lance preceding him.

The troopers heard more Indians yelling before the crash of the thunder drowned everything out. It was no sound to hear when you were alone, in the middle of the night.

The soldiers did their duty as they saw it. They snapped off one shot apiece from their carbines in the general direction of the Indians. Then, by unspoken agreement, they proceeded to reduce the distance between themselves and Fort Sill in the shortest possible time. It may have been that the storm aided their escape, but Dies Young always claimed that the two representatives of the Tenth Cavalry had outrun his horse on foot.

The Indians slipped through the streaming night like bronzed, dripping ghosts. They rounded up seventy-three terrified horses and mules and cut their hobbles. They helped themselves to the two saddled cavalry horses left behind by the troopers in their strategic withdrawal, and that made seventy-five.

It was not a bad night's work.

There was no need for the decoy they had planned. The soldiers from Fort Sill could never find them in the storm; they probably would not even try before morning. Laughing and singing, ignoring the rain, the Comanches and Kiowas herded their stolen stock westward across the mountains, through their ancient lands, the Comancheria, toward the Staked Plains, the country of the Kwahadis.

Truly, it was a night to remember. They pushed away from the rising sun through a black and rain-swept night, six happy men. Buffalo Tongue, his young face bursting with pride, said it for all of them. "Ai-eee," he cried gleefully into the storm. "There will be more walking soldiers at the fort today than there were yesterday!"

It had been a good joke on the *Taibos*.

South of the Canadian and east of the Pecos stretched the *Llano Estacado,* the Staked Plains. That trackless wasteland was shunned even by the buffalo hunters. The slope of the great cap rock that ran from the northeastern corner of the Texas Panhandle to around the New Mexico border divided the known from the unknown. There was no water there, the white men said. Only fools rode out into the Yarner, fools and Comanches.

To Fox Claw, the Staked Plains were a part of home.

A strange land it was, a wild hard land that rolled on forever beneath an endless sky. A beautiful land, if a man could see its beauty. He loved to ride on the Staked Plains and see the edges of the earth. It was freedom; he could ride to the end of time and be lost in immensity, in grandeur.

Water was the riddle of the Staked Plains, the survival puzzle that had to be solved. In all that vast land, no rivers flowed. Sometimes, when the rains had been good, water would gush out of the sides of a draw and the earth would drink it dry. There were water holes, if a man could find them. Sometimes they had water in them and sometimes they didn't. There were times, in this strange land, when the rains made sudden lakes in the shallow basins that waited patiently through the long dry years. Then fantastic birds would fill the sky and sleepy-eyed frogs would croak in the mud.

Some life there always was: great dry rattlesnakes with their diamond markings gray with dust, little lizards that scrabbled out of the shade of the rocks with their creamy throats gulping at the hot air, slow fat horned toads that stared torpidly at the heat waves dancing in the sky. And sometimes, when the grass was green and the winds were cool, the great animals came: brown-black bands of buffalo moving always into the wind, graceful antelope bounding playfully in a soft sea of grass, herds of wild mustangs, their manes flowing against the rose of a late summer sky.

Sometimes, briefly, the land would ripple with an explosive growth of delicate wild flowers that carpeted the earth with waves of gold. A man remembered these things on the Staked Plains; they were rare and precious. Usually there was nothing to rest the eye. It was only a great flat land under a lonely blue sky, a land that was scorched and blasted by the sun. It was a land where the feathery mesquite and the scrub oaks were little more than bushes, a land where the grass was brown and brittle and sparse. The blue northers howled through the gray winter days, and the summer sun roasted the barren stones.

The *Llano Estacado* was many things, and to the Kwahadis, the Antelope band of the Comanches, it was home. The Kwahadis were still as free as the wind, secure in their stronghold where the white men never came. They hunted what they could, they raided the ranches of Texas for horses and cattle, they crossed the Rio Grande and swept over northern Mexico like a prairie blaze. They traded with the Comancheros from New Mexico: ten pounds of coffee for a good horse, a keg of whiskey for a few mules. The Kwahadis were rich—their horse herds numbered in the thousands.

It was a free land, and the Kwahadis were still The People of old.

Fox Claw felt as though an illness had dropped from

his body. His heart was light. He had Watcher to carry him, he had Dies Young to ride by his side. He had horses and mules to bring to the Kwahadis; he had not come with empty hands. His life could be lived again—for a while.

The fires of the Kwahadis burned under the clear, warm stars.

Fox Claw forced down one last swallow of roasted buffalo meat smeared with honey sauce. He was so full that his stomach muscles ached. He had thrown up once, waited a few minutes, and eaten again until he could eat no more. He was stunned with food. A man had to eat when he could, and no man ever got sick eating buffalo meat.

Drowsily, he watched the wife of Broken Bow cooking the big turtle the children had found. She had tossed the turtle into the fire on its back. When the shell began to sizzle and the turtle managed to flop over and crawl out of the fire, she had patiently hit it with a stick and shoved it back into the flames. It took a long time to cook a turtle properly.

Buffalo Tongue had disappeared with one of the Kwahadi girls, and that was as it should be. Fox Claw tried to remember what it was like when he had lived only sixteen summers. It was not easy to remember; those early years all ran together in his mind like a stream that bubbled into a cold, clean pool. He could remember, when he was very young, riding behind his mother on the big pinto mare. Imagine a warrior riding a mare! He could not remember a time when the sensation of a horse under him had been strange. He had always known horses. And he could remember playing *nanipka* in the long afternoons, when he would go over a small hill and wait while the other children hid themselves under buffalo robes, and then he would come back and try to guess who was hidden under each robe. He could remember spending hours stalking one of the green and yellow hummingbirds—how quick they were in the sunlight, how still they hung in the shimmering air when they found a flower! He would shoot them with a split arrow when he was lucky, and hold their warm feathered bodies in his hand, feeling the tiny heart race and die.

He remembered his grandfather telling him the old stories: how Coyote tricked the cow into carrying him across the river in her stomach and how Coyote ate her, and how the turtle got red eyes when the big snake came, and all the wonderful stories that always began the same way: "One day there were a couple of Comanches out looking for trouble and. . . ." He remembered as though it were yesterday the time of his first buffalo hunt. He remembered the day he had seen his vision, high and alone beneath the windswept sky. . . .

Here, it was easy to remember the good things.

It was time for Buffalo Tongue to receive his medicine, his vision. The boy had been lucky in the raid on the corral, but he might not be so lucky next time.

Broken Bow of the Kwahadis, sitting beside him, broke in on his thoughts. "It has been good having you with us," the old man said.

Fox Claw roused himself. "Your thinking is my thinking. It has been good." He paused and then said slowly, almost involuntarily: "But I must go back. Tomorrow, when the sun is high."

"I do not understand you."

Fox Claw stared into the dying flames. He found it hard to reply to the old man. Words did not come easily to his lips. His mind was cloudy with food. He knew only what he felt deep within himself. "There is the boy, Buffalo Tongue. I know a place where he must go."

"That is only a part of what you think. The boy must go alone. That is the way."

"Yes. But I must show him the place." He leaned forward, searching for words. "All this—the stars in the sky, the smell of the fire, the old ways of your people and my people—all this is good. It is right. But I have known these things in other places and other times. I have known them between the two great rivers, the Arkansas and the Rio Grande, and my father before me. Now my father is old and sick. The cattle eat the grass of the buffalo. There are soldiers and *Taibos* hunters on our camping grounds."

"There are no soldiers here."

"No. But I have seen much of them. I have watched them. They will come here in time. And what will the Kwahadis do then?"

Broken Bow smiled. "The Kwahadis will fight."

"Yes, you will fight. I know that. And it may be that I will fight with you when that time comes. But it is in my heart that we need—something else."

"What else can there be?"

Fox Claw had little faith in his own words. "I have spoken to you of Ishatai."

Broken Bow sighed. He looked very old. "I have heard these things before, many times. There have been other shamans, other great dreams. And yet, things are as they are."

"I fear for the truth of what you say. I am unsure in my heart. But this time it may be different. Our need is very great. Why should the Comanches run and hide like the mice when the owl sails across the face of the moon? This is our land, all of it. If Ishatai has truly found the way. . . ."

Broken Bow stood up, his eyes grave. "Go then and hear his words. If they are good words, tell us of them. And if not—come back to us when you will. We will be here."

The old man walked away.

Fox Claw glanced across the fire. Dies Young was already asleep, his great head falling forward on his chest. The camp of the Kwahadis was silent.

Fox Claw stretched out on the ground. The long, hard muscles of his body relaxed. He smiled a little, listening to the heartbeat of the earth.

He slept.

Watcher was frisky that day in the warm April sun; he twitched his ears and tossed his mane like a colt. He would look back at his rider every now and then, rolling his great liquid eye, as though calling to him: "Come on! Let's go! Let's race the wind!"

Fox Claw responded to Watcher's mood. It *was* a good day, warm but not hot, with plenty of water from the rains and a sprinkle of new green dotting the rolling land.

He felt a nameless hope rising in him like a song. Dies Young rode at his side. Tenebeka and Black Bear and White Horse of the Kiowas jogged along behind them, speaking in sign of the things they saw around them. Buffalo Tongue was wrapped up in himself, reliving the raid and the nights with the Kwahadis. He was very different from the confused and uncertain boy Fox Claw had known on the reservation.

They rode to the northeast under a clean blue sky and gradually the land changed. The almost flat tableland of the Staked Plains gave way to the broken country of the breaks where the great rivers were born: a twisted, rough world of blown sand and jutting rocks, where gray-brown canyons slashed the earth and sentinel buttes reared their stone heads into the high searching winds.

They were getting close to Spirit Hill.

Remember? It had been so long ago. Did the buffalo still wait on Spirit Hill, or had he vanished with so many other lost things? Could the boy hear the Voice that had spoken to Fox Claw, long ago in another world?

While there was still light, they made camp in a grove of cottonwoods. There was good springwater and grass for the horses. Already, the doves were calling in the trees. Fox Claw knew the place of old. It had not changed.

They built no fires, but the evening was warm and pleasant in this sheltered spot. They had good pemmican in their parfleches. The dried buffalo meat mixed with pecans and tallow was a good enough meal for any man.

Fox Claw waited for the darkness. Then he called Buffalo Tongue to his side. "We are here, *tua*," he said.

The boy nodded. "I am ready."

"It was from this very place, many years ago, that I set out for Spirit Hill. The signs, I think, are good. It is less than a day's ride from here. Can you find it?"

"I am not sure. I will try."

"You follow this stream toward the Red River until you come to the two hills that rise above the plains like the breasts of a woman. The hill that looks down upon the other is Spirit Hill. It has the power in it."

"I will not fail again."

"No, *tua*, this time you will not fail. Here. I have

brought these things for you." He gave Buffalo Tongue a bone pipe, tobacco, and an old fire drill in a case of buffalo horn. The boy had a good buffalo robe of his own. "Tonight, you will cleanse yourself in the spring. In the morning, you will go."

"I will not come back without the *puha*, the power. I swear it!"

Fox Claw's sharp-lined face was dark and grim in the starlight. "I never had a son of my own, *tua*. Be sure you come back. Do not take risks. There are many soldiers in this country. You will be weak from the fasting. . . ."

"A man must go alone when he seeks the vision," the boy said. "The soldiers cannot harm me when I have my medicine."

"So it is said." Fox Claw wanted to tell him that he had seen many men die who had good medicine. But he could not say that to him now. And the medicine of Spirit Hill was strong, strong, "You must take great care."

Buffalo Tongue was excited. He was in no mood to listen to words of caution. "I will not forget what you have told me. Now, I must go to the spring and make myself ready."

Fox Claw watched the boy as he almost ran toward the water. Then, slowly, he went over to sit by Dies Young. It was time for Buffalo Tongue to be alone. He had done all he could do.

In the morning, when he opened his eyes to the raucous call of a fat jay in the cottonwoods, the boy was gone.

Curtis

Curtis waved the column to a halt at the Dawson place and swung stiffly out of the saddle. His shoulders ached and his temper was short with frustration, but he put a confident smile on his face. The Dawsons had enough to worry about without his adding to their troubles.

Kenneth was the first one to him. He was a tow-headed kid of fifteen, all arms and legs and big blue eyes. The boy was so excited at the sight of the cavalry that he could hardly speak.

Curtis inspected him gravely and extended his hand. Kenneth did a man's work and did not like to be treated as a child. "Good to see you again, Kenneth. How are things going?"

Kenneth met his gaze evenly. "Fine, sir. Can you come in and set?" He tried to keep his voice low and resonant, but it betrayed him from time to time.

"Not this time, I'm afraid."

"Out after Injuns?"

"Something like that. Your folks at home?"

"Pa's out doctoring a heifer. Ma's in the kitchen."

"Thank you, Kenneth. Here, you have a talk with Captain Irvine, will you? I just want to say hello to your mother."

Matt moved in and collected the boy. Kenneth's eyes widened with unabashed hero-worship. Matt had a way with kids. He gave the boy a drink from his canteen. The water was warm and stale, but Kenneth drank it eagerly.

Curtis walked across the bare hen yard to the little square sod-roofed house in the middle of nowhere. Judith Dawson met him at the door.

Curtis took off his hat. "Mrs. Dawson," he said, smiling. "Kenneth tells me Paul's not here."

"He'll be back shortly. Please come in, Bill."

"Can't do that. Wish I could. Just passing by." Curtis looked at her with admiration. Judith Dawson was not a pretty woman, although she might have been under different circumstances. She was tall and thin, with the soft blue eyes of her son. Her hands were work-reddened and her blonde hair was tied carelessly with a faded blue scarf. She was just about the bravest woman Curtis had ever known, and he had never heard her complain.

"Trouble, Bill?"

"Not exactly, but I'd feel a whole lot better if you would move in closer to town for a while."

"Paul won't go," she said simply.

"I know that." Curtis slapped his knee with his hat. He took a deep breath. "Little trouble at Sill. Some Indians ran off with a bunch of horses. Nothing to worry you about. Has Paul seen any sign?"

Judith Dawson smoothed her cotton dress. "There hasn't been a thing. It's been very quiet. I wish you'd stay." She smiled. "We could use some company."

"Another time, Judith. I've got a whole column out here. They'd drink your well dry."

"Your men are welcome to water, you know that."

"Yes. I know." Curtis did not want to leave. He always felt as though he were abandoning the Dawsons when he left. But Paul Dawson was a stubborn man. God knew why he had chosen this place to live, but it was his and he meant to stay. "Tell Paul I dropped by."

Judith Dawson nodded. She did not ask him to delay again.

Curtis walked back to his horse and took the reins from his striker. He waved to Kenneth. "Take care of your mother," he said.

"I will," the boy said seriously. "Good-bye, sir. So long, Captain Irvine."

"Take it easy, Kenneth," Matt said. "I'll bring you that old shotgun next time I get out this way."

"You won't forget?"

"I won't forget."

Curtis climbed back into the saddle and motioned to Jim and the Tonk scouts to move out. He gave them a good lead and then gave the signal for the column to move forward.

He did not look back at the Dawson place as he rode away. Even in broad daylight, the little ranch seemed exposed and forlorn. He knew how it was at night. A couple of coal-oil lamps burning against the darkness. There were a lot of nights at the Dawson place, and the nights were long. The sod-roofed house was tiny under the stars, a fly-speck set down in emptiness, lonely and lost. . . .

The horses were kicking up dust again—not the choking white clouds of summer dust, but dust for all of that. It was amazing how quickly this land could dry out. Sheets of cold green-tinted water had covered the plains after the storms. Then the water turned to sticky mud that clung in great gobs to the hooves of the horses, and then the sun had gone to work. It was a powerful sun, that Texas sun: it could hit you like a fist. The bare earth cracked in long fissure lines, and soon it was as dry as an old white bone in a waterless cave. The big cavalry horses kicked up the dust in explosive little puffs and the fine grains settled on the faded blue uniforms and sifted into a man's hair and shoes. A man always had the taste of grit in his mouth. He could grind the grains between his teeth.

Curtis had A Company and C Company with him, one hundred and twenty men. He was three days out of Fort Wade. They had been three days of complete futility. The only Indians Curtis had seen had been his own Tonk scouts.

He was disgusted with Davidson. It was a direct insult to the army to permit those Indians to run off with the horses from the Sill corral. Yes, and it was dangerous to let the Indians get the notion that they could play around with the army. The power of the army depended largely on fear; there weren't enough men to watch everywhere at once. He didn't blame the Negro soldiers at Sill; they were good troopers. It was a command failure, and that put it at Davidson's door.

This sort of shadowboxing always magnified the irritations of a campaign. Chasing phantoms in empty country was one hell of a way to build up morale, his own included. He knew that the men were in a bad temper. They were taking it out on Lieutenant Pease. Pease, despite his beard, was having trouble living up to his own vision of a gallant cavalry officer. He had picked up a dandy case of the runs, and that could be murder to a man being jolted around on a saddle. Pease had to dismount with annoying frequency and hide behind scattered clumps of mesquite while the troopers made knowing cracks about the gutty products of West Point. Someday, if he lived, Pease would gather his kids around him and tell about the great days of the Indian wars, and he probably would have forgotten all about the gut cramps. But right now it was one bush at a time.

Captain Taylor of C Company had withdrawn into a position of accusing silence. Even Matt Irvine had hinted that they might as well go back to the fort.

Well, the devil with them. Curtis wasn't ready to go back. He had failed to intercept the Indians with their stolen stock—that was clear enough. But he still had a chance to head them off on their way back to the reservation.

If they came this way. And *if* they went back to the reservation at all. And *if* he was lucky.

He didn't even know which Indians he was looking for, not that that was unusual. There was no way to check to find out who was on the reservation and who had flown the coop. Even the agent, Samuel Reed, wouldn't know or wouldn't tell. Comanches, Davidson had said, but how could he be certain? And if they had been Comanches, which Comanches? Quanah, the son of Cynthia Ann Parker who had become an Indian war leader? Shaking Hand? How about old Satanta of the Kiowas? He didn't have the faintest clue to their identity.

The final irony, of course, was that the raiders would not know *his* name either. It was one hell of a strange war.

Curtis pulled his hat down more firmly on his head.

He meant to find the Indians if it was humanly possible.

He didn't give a damn how long it took.

Buffalo Tongue

The boy was afraid.

Since there were none to see, he did not try to hide his fear. He twisted in his saddle from time to time, looking behind him. He spoke strong medicine words into the wind.

Four times that day he had stopped to offer smoke

and prayer to the Spirit, and now the day was dying. The Sun, who was himself a great god, was sinking into the west, the land of the dead. Before him, the two hills lifted some three hundred feet into the air, their crests still touched with gold. Buffalo Tongue felt the tension of power in the shadowed air; it made it seem colder than it was.

Spirit Hill—he could not mistake it—loomed up ahead of him in silent challenge. It was a challenge to his faith as well as to his courage, a challenge only dimly grasped, half understood, felt with the senses rather than the mind. Ai-eee, was it not said that the Thunderbird lived in such a place, on such a hill? The Thunderbird that was immense and colored dark blue with the jagged red markings that were shaped like the lightning that ripped the sky? Had he not seen for himself that sacred spot, not far from here on the Red River, where the Thunderbird had touched the earth? There was a mark there—he remembered it vividly—a charred place where no grass ever grew. A mark in the shape of a giant bird with wings outstretched. Ah, with his own eyes he had seen this thing!

The gathering night seemed filled with the dark winds of invisible wings. Buffalo Tongue tried to be brave, but it was hard to be brave when you were alone. It was easier to be brave when others rode at your side. It was easier to be brave after you had the medicine that would protect you and shield you from harm.

He did not even consider turning back. There was only one way to go if he wanted to become a man, a man with horses of his own, and a wife, and the respect of The People.

He had to go up Spirit Hill.

He rode his pony between the two hills, into a small sheltered valley. There was a small spring there, just as Fox Claw had said, and enough grass for many days. He unsaddled his horse and staked him out on a long rope. "I will be back for you, Ekaesi," he whispered into the ear of the red roan. "Wait here for me. Wait here for me and you will carry a warrior away from this place. We have hunted together many times, but this is a kind of hunting a man must do alone. Do you understand my words, Ekaesi?"

The roan nuzzled him affectionately. "I am glad that you are here," the boy said softly. "I will look down upon you and see you when I am too much alone, and my heart will be glad."

Reluctantly, he left the horse he had raised from a colt. He gathered up his buffalo robe, his tobacco and pipe, and his fire drill in its case of buffalo horn. He started up Spirit Hill.

It was not a hard climb, but he was not used to climbing on foot and his heart hammered in his chest. The wind stirred through the brush and the great rocks took on strange and fearful shapes. The Sun could not see him now and the air was filled with tiny cold teeth. Once, his foot dislodged a stone and it went bouncing down into the valley below; to the boy, it sounded like a landslide.

He reached the top. It was perfectly level, a flat cap rock some thirty yards across. Nothing grew there except four stunted, wind-sculptured cedars that had found purchase in a crevice on the south side. Four cedars! That was the medicine number.

Buffalo Tongue felt cold sweat on his hands. He could see for miles in every direction. Earth, the Mother, the guardian of the young, was below him: dark she was, and without color, but wrapped in a cloth of silver. Over him and around him was the night, filled now with the warm blaze of the stars. It came to him that this place stood outside of time, beyond time; it had waited here forever between the sky and the earth, waited here before The People had come out of the north, waited here before the buffalo were born. It had been the same when Fox Claw had come, and all the others who had come before Fox Claw. It would be the same for his sons, when he had sons. It would always be here, waiting, for those who could find it and use it. . . .

He did not know how long he stood there. But it seemed only a short time before the Moon rose above the rim of the world. It was big, bigger than he had ever seen it, fat and yellow and marked with strange dark lines. The Moon too was a Mother, the guardian of the warriors on a raid. He managed a smile. He told himself that he was not alone. He had Ekaesi below him and Mother Moon above him. And there were others, somewhere, watching.

He watched the Moon for a long time, watched it change into a small silver ball, watched it climb high into the night and float among the stars. The night was very clear, and very still. The only sound was the rustle of the wind.

Buffalo Tongue moved very carefully, making sure that he did all the right things. This time, there must be no mistake. He carried his buffalo robe to the south side of the cap rock, almost to the four cedar trees. He lay down on the stone, facing the east, and covered himself with the robe. He tried to sleep. That was the way.

He found that sleep was slow in coming. He could not forget where he was. The stories he had heard, the things that had happened in this place....

How would his vision come to him? In the scream of an eagle, the cry of a wolf? Ah, the wolf medicine was good. No bullet could harm a man who was guarded by the wolf; only an arrow could be dangerous, and the soldiers had no arrows. Or it could be a Voice that spoke to him in the night—perhaps this very night—a Voice that gave him instructions and signs to watch for. Many of his friends had heard the Voice. Or it might be that the Thunderbird would roar over this place, and the heavens would light with fire—

He could not know. He would have to wait. But he could feel the forces around him in the night, hear them whispering in the black cedars. He would not fail again. He must not even think of failure.

He closed his eyes.

Somehow, sleep came to him—and then, suddenly, it was morning.

His eyes opened into the glare of the Sun. At once, he threw aside the robe that had covered him. He got to his feet. He stood facing the Sun, staring straight at it with narrowed eyes. He extended his hands, palms upward, reaching out for the sky. He felt the power of the Sun: the Sun was a god that warmed him and filled his body with strength and health. How strange it was—the warmth seemed to well up within him, moving out to the Sun, answering the Sun. It was good. He knew that it was a good sign.

He filled his bone pipe with tobacco that was as dry as dust. He took out his fire drill and tamped the tinder of dry Spanish moss into the hole in the wooden drill block. He inserted the hardwood drill into the hole and began to twirl it between the palms of his hands. It was a slow process and he sang to himself as he worked. Finally, a little smoke curled up from the edges of the hole, and then the tinder caught. Instantly, he removed the hardwood drill and scooped up the burning moss with his bare hand, putting it into the bowl of his pipe. He puffed carefully on the stem until the tobacco caught. He offered the pipe to the Sun and then to the Earth Mother and then to the four directions. He smoked and prayed until the tobacco in the bowl gave out. There were easier ways of making a fire, of course, but the old ways were best when a man was seeking power. The taste of the dry smoke was unpleasant, though; it made him thirsty.

There was nothing more he could do. He had to wait.

The Sun climbed high into the sky. He did not doubt that the Sun was a god and would help him, but just the same it got uncomfortably hot on top of Spirit Hill. The stunted cedars gave little shade. The winds swept across the great empty spaces and dried his skin, but the winds did not cool him. All that day he sat motionless on the cap rock. He ate no food and drank no water. The hours crawled by. That night he slept more easily, and in the morning he smoked and prayed again.

Nothing happened.

The hunger did not bother him much; he was used to hunger. But the heat and the dry wind sucked out his juices. His lips cracked and his throat turned raw. When he tried to swallow, there was nothing there. He thought less of visions and more of the little spring at the foot of Spirit Hill. He could not quite see the spring when he walked to the edge of the cap rock to look at his horse, but he could smell it. It had a green smell, the smell of fresh living grass, and it was moist and cool, cool . . . .

The day passed, and the night. On the afternoon of the third day, he had to move, had to do something. He would not have believed that time could pass so slowly. He climbed back down the slope of Spirit Hill; his legs were weak and twice he stumbled. He tried to talk to Ekaesi but no words would come from his cracked and bleeding lips. He went to the tiny spring and stared at it, drinking it with his eyes. He plunged his dusty head into the little pool. The shock of the water almost made him faint. He let it soak his hair and soothe the burning in the skin of his face. He opened his mouth and tasted the water with his parched tongue—sweet, cold water.

But he did not drink.

He turned away from the spring and made his way back up Spirit Hill. It was very hard going now; he was light-headed and dizzy and he seemed to have no control over his arms and legs. He fell before he reached the top. He pulled himself up on his hands and knees and crawled the last few feet to the cap rock. He dragged himself out into the white glare of the sunlight. The scorched rock scraped his chest and he left a slight, fast-drying trail of crimson behind him. The crimson quickly faded to brown in the sun.

He felt it when the Sun dropped down in the land of the dead; he could not watch it with his eyes. The evening breeze was cooler and revived him a little. He sat on the still hot stone. He was giddy and shook his head to clear it.

Listen!

He thought he could hear something.

He strained his ears, listening. Was that a Voice, whispering to him from the dead land beyond the grave of the Sun?

No. He could not fool himself. It was the wind, only the wind . . . .

He crawled under the buffalo robe, trembling. He was hot but he knew that he would be chilled when he slept. This was the fourth night, the last night. Tomorrow would be the final day. If he saw no sign—

Do not think of it. Do not think of it.

His thoughts raced on: he could not stop them. What if the old gods had lost their power? What if the medicine could not come? So many things had changed. He was young; he had never seen the old days. Was it all a lie? Or was it only a dream, that time when the earth was free and The People rode with the wind? If he failed now, what could he do? What would happen to him?

He felt the stars burning into him, and then the Moon. Mother Moon, guardian of warriors. Ah, her light was soft and cool and silver this night. She eased his hurts.

Look down on me, Mother Moon. Help me, my heart is crying . . . .

He must have slept, for suddenly he was aware that he had awakened.

His first impression was one of light, light all around him. It was a strange light, it was a glow of silver-gold that seemed to fill the air and wash the rocks of Spirit Hill with radiance. He had never seen anything like it. He pushed aside the buffalo robe and struggled to his feet. Had the night ended? Was this the dawn? He did not know. Everything was different, changed, transformed. Every detail was vivid before his eyes: the twisted cedars, the sweep of the land below, the tiny cracks in the cap rock. The world was bathed in a magic light. It was a new world, a world he had never known.

An older world?

With shaking hands he twirled fire into being and lit his pipe. The smoke made his head swim. He offered the pipe to the silver-gold sky, to the Earth Mother below, to the north and the south and the west and—

And there it was.

Suddenly, quietly, it was there. He dropped his pipe; it clattered on the stone. A bull buffalo stood silently on the eastern edge of the cap rock, where no buffalo could ever be. It was a real buffalo, not a dream. He stared at it, transfixed. The long black-brown hair of the buffalo's head and neck was thick and luxuriant. The animal's weak red eyes looked straight at the boy in the strange light. His short white horns came to tiny sharp points that gleamed like stars. A curl of white spittle dripped down from the left side of his hard mouth into his dark beard. His shoulders and hump were enormous; they were like mountains. His little tufted tail twitched slightly. The boy could hear him breathing, distinctly. He could smell his sour breath and his warm, heavy animal scent.

He heard the Voice.

The Voice spoke in his head. It was not loud, but every word was clear.

Remember me. I am the Buffalo who gave to you your name. I am your power and your guardian spirit. I will be with you always. I will protect you and make you strong. You need have no fears. You will sing the Buffalo Song when you need me and I will hear. Listen to my words. You are to make a medicine bag. Into this bag you will place sweet grass and the claws of an eagle. Into this bag you will place also a buffalo stone for power, which you shall find where I have stood. You will carry this bag with you always. I am the Buffalo who gave to you your name. Remember me.

The boy blinked his eyes and the buffalo was gone. Shaking with excitement, he ran across the cap rock to where the buffalo had been. He fell to his hands and knees, searching frantically. Ai-eee, there it was! A drop of spittle where the buffalo had stood; yes, he was certain of it, it was still wet to his touch. And there—a small smooth white stone. A buffalo stone from the stomach of the buffalo! He had seen many such in his lifetime—there was no mistaking it.

It was real. *It was real*. That stone could not possibly have been here before on top of Spirit Hill. He would have seen it, as would have the others before him. The stone was hard and warm and unyielding in his hand; he gripped it tightly. It was real!

The boy stood up, his heart hammering against his ribs. The strange silver-gold light was gone. A new light flooded the cap rock and the lands below, the pure soft light of dawn. The Father Sun lifted above the rim of the earth, framing the place where the buffalo had stood.

It was over. He had not failed.

He scooped up his robe and his pipe and his fire-drill case, still clutching the buffalo stone in his right hand. He scrambled down the side of Spirit Hill, almost running in his eagerness. He fell once, skinning his knee, but he hardly noticed it. His horse nickered when he saw him and the boy threw his arms around the roan's sleek neck, dropping everything to the ground except the hard white stone.

"Ekaesi, Ekaesi. You have a man to carry."

He fumbled out a strip of pemmican from the parfleche with his saddle. He carried it to the tiny spring. He fell down on his belly and dipped his head into the night-cold water. He opened his dry mouth and drank. The water poured into his parched body like a river of ice. It stabbed at his insides. No matter! He drank his fill. He rolled over, luxuriating in the sweet grass. He began to chew his pemmican. He ate as much as he could choke down, but he could not finish the dried meat. His stomach cramped in pain.

Buffalo Tongue lay there in the morning sun, completely exhausted. The roan walked up and nuzzled him. He closed his eyes. His stomach hurt him terribly but that was nothing. His happiness was too big for pain.

He would rest until he was stronger. Yes, that was the way. There was no need to hurry. He had a lifetime of years ahead of him. He could spend this day by the spring, drinking whenever he wished. He could finish the pemmican, in time. His strength would come back.

He would ride to the reservation with the news. He would tell Fox Claw and his father. He was a man!

He lay quite still, waiting for the cramping to stop. He held the buffalo stone tightly in his hand. The day was good, everything was good.

He slept, and in his sleep he smiled.

Curtis

It had been more than a week since the two companies of the Twelfth Cavalry had left Fort Wade. They had moved out into the Panhandle plains country with guidons flying and sabers clanking. The big troop horses had been rested and eager. The men were full of beans and high spirits. Curtis remembered that they had actually been singing that first spring day, yelling out that little ditty that was aimed at General Crook, who avoided a uniform like the plague and nursed his ornery mules along like a mother hen with her chicks:

"I'd like to be a packer,
And pack with George F. Crook,
"And dressed up in my canvas suit,
To be for him mistook.
"I'd braid my beard in two long tails,
And idle all the day
"In whittling sticks and wondering
What the New York papers say."

On the second day out, the men had been singing a new song, composed for the occasion by a scrupulously anonymous trooper who had not been moved to tears by the intestinal plight of Lieutenant Pease:

"There was Colonel William Curtis
and natty Captain Matt, hey
"Oh, they made us ride where the
Injuns hide in good old Company A.
"Oh, the lieutenant would ROLL! Upon
my soul, this is the style we'd go:
"Forty miles a day on dust and hay in
the Regular Army O!"

After the third day, when they had stopped at the Dawson place, there had been no more singing. If there had been any new songs, which Curtis thought likely, they had not been judged fit for the ears of officers. One hundred and twenty tired and dirty men had ridden back and forth across an empty sun-drenched land. They had forded the high waters of the Canadian, the Washita, the North Fork of the Red, and the Red River itself. That was all. The men were disgusted. Curtis was aware of his own edgy mood and restrained himself from snapping at his men for minor offenses.

The entire command was in a raw, red mood. It wasn't a serious situation, if a man could view it with objectivity. There was no thought of mutiny or desertion or anything of that kind. But Curtis was in the middle of it, and objectivity was far away. He felt the undercurrents all around him: they were tangible, real. There was an air of saw-toothed irritability made up of a host of small annoyances: cracked lips, dust in the hair, flopping carbine slings rubbing against the chest, hats that blew off in the wind, saddle rashes, lame horses, tepid canteen water that tasted like sweaty socks. The men were spoiling for trouble, any trouble, and so was Curtis.

When they spotted the Indian on the eighth day out, a shock of excitement ran through the column like a shaft of welcome lightning. The hunters had found their game.

It was just one Indian, and he was utterly alone as far as Curtis could see, a solitary figure on the hot empty plains. He was jogging along in the general direction of Fort Sill and he was taking his time. At first, the Indian seemed not to see the dust cloud kicked up by the cavalry patrol behind him. He just went on riding at an easy walk, his roan horse blending in with the mesquite and the brush and the yellow-brown earth. From all outward appearances, he hadn't a care in the world.

Curtis lifted his hand and halted his command. Matt Irvine reined in at his side and Captain Taylor of C Company joined them. The three officers studied the situation for a long minute.

"Well, Matt?"

Matt Irvine grinned and pulled at his bedraggled mustache. "Well, sir, it's an Injun, that I know. I figure that's what we've been blisterin' our eyeballs trying to find."

"Captain Taylor?"

Taylor—a small man, almost dapper despite the dust that covered him from head to foot—shrugged. "He's almost certainly alone, I would say. If that's a Kiowa or a Comanche we ought to hightail it after him. Could be that the horse thieves have split up and are trying to ride in one at a time. If that's so, this will be our only chance at them."

Curtis held himself in check. He thought it out. He was not about to rush into anything half-cocked, not in this country. "He might not be alone, gentlemen. This country has enough roll in it to hide a whole damned tribe off there somewhere. I don't propose to fall for the oldest trick in the book."

"I think he's alone, Colonel," Matt said.

"Yes, I think so too—but we've got to be ready in case we're mistaken. Very well. Have the men form two lines. Captain Irvine and A Company will lead. Captain Taylor and C Company will follow at a distance of fifty yards. Instruct the men that the Indian is to be given every chance to surrender if he chooses. If he resists, A Company is to open fire. Got that?"

The two officers nodded, impatiently.

"Very well. If there are more Indians up ahead and he's a decoy to suck us into a trap, I want no mistakes. I will tolerate no mistakes. There are no natural fortifications here; this is pretty level ground. If we are attacked, the entire command will abandon the chase *at once* and make a full turn to the left. We will continue until the bugler sounds halt. Captain Irvine and A Company will form a skirmish line. Captain Taylor and C Company will regroup around the back of the skirmish line and await further orders. Is this understood?"

"Got it, sir," Matt said.

"Captain Taylor?"

"Understood, sir."

Curtis smiled. "Very good. Instruct your men. Send the bugler to me and I will signal the charge. Good luck, gentlemen."

A minute and a half later, Curtis lifted his saber. He felt a little foolish in taking such elaborate precautions against what seemed to be a single Indian. But he had learned that it was better to hedge his bets than to risk a massacre.

The bugler sounded the clipped, rapid piercing notes of *Charge!*

The Twelfth leapt to the attack.

It was a release, an explosion of pent-up emotions. No matter how many times it happened, it was always an incomparable thrill. No doubts now, no hesitations! There was nothing like a cavalry charge—there had never been anything like it, and never would be again. Curtis felt his whole being lifted up, carried along with a force and fury that was nameless, elemental. His own voice was only one of many; every man in the outfit was screaming at the top of his lungs. The horses beat a solid tattoo on the hard earth, an unforgettable cascade of sound, a drumming roar that hurtled across the plains like a mammoth wall of water from a suddenly shattered dam. The guidons and standards snapped in the wind, the yellow dust boiled up behind them in seething mountains of dirt.

Nothing could stand before that charge. Nothing!

Curtis knew that he couldn't stop it now if he wanted to. The sheer momentum of the charge carried it out of control, or seemed to; it would ride over anything in its path. Later, this might worry Curtis—but not now.

He spurred his horse wildly. His saber cut the wind. "Get him!" he heard himself yelling. "Get him, get him, get him!"

The Indian looked back once and kicked his roan pony into action. He dropped low along the neck of his horse and the horse responded with a desperate gallop. He had a fair lead, but it wasn't good enough. The big troop horses narrowed the gap steadily. The Indian somehow managed to get to his rifle. He twisted in his saddle and loosed one wild shot at the oncoming avalanche of horses.

The troopers hollered louder. Curtis grinned. He was glad that the Indian had fired. That made it final, that absolved him from any responsibility. . . .

A Company opened up. The big Springfields cracked out in a thin jagged wall of fire, the sounds almost lost in the roar of the thudding hooves. The roan pony stumbled and went down, throwing the Indian clear. He hit and rolled. He tried to get to his feet—

The Twelfth rode him down. The first wave galloped over him with sabers swinging. When C Company hit, the body was hacked apart.

It was a great victory.

It took a long time to halt the charge. The horses

were running flat out, and the realization that there was nothing more to fight was slow in coming. The horses were wild-eyed and snorting. The men were scarcely different.

Curtis managed to circle back. He jerked his mount to a stop and dismounted. He stared down at the thing that had been a man and the wildness in his blood turned to water.

Well, he thought, *it was a Comanche. That's something.*

He knelt and touched the body. It was still warm, still bleeding, staining the earth. How thin he was, all skin and bones. . . .

Matt Irvine rode up. He sat in his saddle, looking. "Just a kid," he said.

"We hit him pretty fast," Curtis said.

"He's plenty old enough to kill," Matt said flatly. "No harm done. He was probably one of 'em."

"Yes. No harm done."

Curtis found it hard to tear himself away. A little shiver ran through the mutilated corpse. The fingers of the boy's left hand loosened. A small hard white stone rolled onto the trampled earth.

"Buffalo stone," Matt said. "Big medicine."

Curtis stood up. "Didn't help him much, did it?"

"Reckon not."

"See to a burial detail, Matt. Put him under."

Curtis remounted. He was surprised to find that he was trembling. It was probably just the aftermath of the charge. Hell, there was no reason to blame himself. He had his men to think of. There might have been hundreds of Indians concealed in the rolling plains, waiting. Command decisions were never easy. A man could never be *sure*.

He looked around him. His eyes went through the milling riders without seeing them. He did not hear the buzz of excited voices, the blowing of the horses. He looked out at the plains, and the plains were vast and empty and silent under the sun.

Curtis felt better, and he did not like himself for it. The tension in him was gone. *Maybe that's all it takes,* he thought. *A killing. One killing. One boy cut up like a pig.*

He had to face it. He had enjoyed it.

Still, he wished that there had been more than one. He had been ready for a fight. He needed a fight.

One thing that rankled, of course, was the seeming foolishness of charging a lone Indian with two full companies of cavalry. He knew that he already had a nickname with his men: Company Curtis. There were those who said that he was unaware that platoons existed, to say nothing of squads. Yes, and there were those who said that the commanding officer should stay behind in the fort instead of leading patrols all over the plains.

Well, to hell with them. Curtis had faith in his judgment. If you had power, you used it. It was stupid to risk lives if you didn't have to. It was his job to win and he intended to keep on winning. As for staying behind in his command post—he could not do it, and that was that. He was lucky to have the major part of his regiment together at Wade instead of just a fragment of it; the fort was properly defended even with two full companies out. In any event, he could not imagine the Indians making a frontal assault on Wade. The idea was fantastic.

He had done well. There was no reason to worry.

Captain Taylor reined in beside him. He was beaming with satisfaction. "Well," he said, "we got one of them. That's something."

"Yes," Curtis said. "That's something."

Ishatai

Ishatai was young in years, but there were other ways of counting time. It seemed to him that he had always been different from other men, had always stood a little apart from them. At first, this had caused him much unhappiness. It was not easy to be different, and the choice had not been his. It had been hard for Ishatai, as a child, to look out from the shadows of his father's tepee and see the other boys playing their games without him. In later years, it had hurt him to see the fear looking out at him from the dark eyes of the women. Time had passed slowly for Ishatai. When he had finally accepted the fact of his difference, his life began to take on meaning.

He remembered something that his father had once told him. His father had been a great doctor; Ishatai had grown up surrounded by the smells of sickness and the paraphernalia of healing: stones for the sweat lodge, eagle and crow feathers, sweet grass and herbs, buffalo tails, splints, horn sucking tubes, medicine bones from *piamempits*, the Cannibal Owl. "My son," his father had said, "we are alike, you and I. I wouldn't have wished it for you, but it is so. I can see the signs in your eyes. Your road will be long and hard. But one day the power will come to you, as it came to me. You will know how it is to live in two worlds, the world of The People and the world of the spirits. You will know great sadness. But you will also know of things that others cannot know—hidden things, dark and powerful things. It is a fair bargain. Learn to walk your own path wherever it leads, and be unafraid." His father had smiled then, and he was very gentle and very near. "There are some things which I can show you. They will ease your way. You will have your own good life in time, Ishatai. Remember my words. Do not despair."

Ishatai had not forgotten. He had learned his lessons well. At first, there had been tricks. He learned how to hide the hair ball in his mouth while he prepared the sucking tube, how to throw his voice into the back of the tepee, how to grip small stones in the palms of his hands where they could not be seen. Then he had learned the humble arts of healing—how to set a broken bone, how to stop bleeding, how to mend a tooth cavity with dried mushrooms.

And then, as his father had foretold, his true power had come.

Ishatai had died from a raging fever; his spirit had plunged into a red-shot blackness from which there was no return. And yet he had come back to life again. He had seen strange things while he was in the land of the dead, things which would stay with him always. He had looked into the unearthly eyes of his father when he was born again, and he had seen those same memories in the depths of his father's eyes. Years later, he had seen the great fireball that moved through the sky. A great knowledge had come to him. He had told The People that the fireball would last for five days and then disappear forever. He had told them that the coming summer would be very dry.

The People had laughed at him. But the fireball went away as he had said, and the summer had indeed been dry. It had not rained for five months. The People never laughed at him again.

Ishatai discovered that there were compensations for being different. There was always good food in his tepee. He received many gifts and many horses. And if women did not love him, he yet had ways of bringing women to him.

His life became easier. There were those who envied him. Ishatai learned pride.

Then the thing had happened. His life, if it had ever been his own, was taken out of his hands. His uncle, who had always been kind to Ishatai, was killed by the white-eyes under Lieutenant Hudson of the Fourth Cavalry. Ishatai had been hurt and shamed; his uncle had been under his protection.

Ishatai vowed vengeance. He fasted for many days. He called on all the powers he knew. He drifted down the river of dreams, he came close again the land of the dead. . . .

Ishatai had a mighty vision. It was so much more than he had expected that it had shaken him. It was a vision of hope, not of despair, and it was so strong that it had left him sick and dizzy for many days. Ishatai had been where no man had been before him and from that moment he was changed forever.

It was not a vision for him alone. It was not a vision for private vengeance. It was a vision given to him for all The People. It was the greatest vision a man could have.

He saw it clearly, precisely, without shadows. He could never tell about it in all its wonder, but he knew what he had seen.

He had climbed into the blue sky and floated above the clouds. He had actually walked on the tops of the clouds; the clouds had swirled like white smoke over his moccasins. He had climbed and climbed, walking up the sky, until even the eagles were as tiny as flies below him. He had climbed and climbed, and he had stretched out his hands—

Ishatai saw the Spirit.

The Spirit was brighter than the Sun. Ishatai covered his eyes and still he saw the Spirit. The Spirit spoke to him and the words roared like thunder in his ears.

"Ishatai!"

Ishatai could not speak. The roar of the Voice struck at him: he was afraid that he would fall through the sky.

"Ishatai!"

Four times the Spirit spoke his name, and four times Ishatai could not reply.

The Voice changed. It became soft, the whisper of the wind. He had to strain to hear it. "Listen to my words, O Ishatai, and carry them to The People. I have been watching. I have always been watching, and I do not like what I have seen. Listen!"

Ishatai could not move. He was frozen in the caverns of the sky.

"You can see what I have seen," the Voice whispered in his ears. "You can see that the Indians who have tried to follow the way of the white men are perishing, just as a wolf must die if he tries to live as a snake. With each passing day, the Indians are fewer. With each passing day, the Indians are poorer. Look at them! Can you not see that the Caddos and the Wichitas are wrapped in misery? Can you not see that The People themselves are weakening and sickening on the reservation? Listen! I say to you that The People were meant to be free! They must not walk further down the white man's road. That road leads only to despair and destruction. The People must walk their own path again."

Ishatai could not speak his question, but the Spirit heard it.

The Voice roared again like thunder; it filled the sky. "Kill the white men, burn them from the earth! I will give you the power. They cannot stand against me. Kill the white men, and all will be as it once was. The buffalo will come back! The People will be strong. The grass will grow tall and the rivers will run with sweet cold water. The People will be free! Listen! To you, Ishatai, who have had the courage to walk the ancient path, I give strong medicine. I tell you that when you ride in a battle the bullets of the white men will fall like mud from the muzzles of their guns. You cannot be killed by them, and those that ride with you cannot be killed by them. I give you the power. Believe!"

I believe.

"Listen!" The Voice was the sound of the night wind in the cottonwoods. "This is the way. Never before have The People had a Sun Dance like that of their brothers, the Kiowas. Never have all of The People gathered together in one place and felt of their might. It is for you, Ishatai, to do these things. Call in The People from their scattered camps! Hold the Sun Dance as the Kiowas do! The People will hear your words, for they are my words. Other Indians will join you. You are strong, not weak! You cannot be killed by the white men. The white men will be driven from this land, never to return. You can bring back the dead warriors of The People, for I give to you this power. Remember my words, O Ishatai! I will send you a sign when the time is right. You will not fail!" The Voice grew faint and far away. The light grew weaker. "Listen and remember, listen and remember . . . ."

The Spirit was gone.

Ishatai was shaking with fear. He wanted to lie down but he did not dare. Slowly, carefully, he started his descent through the clouds. The white clouds fastened themselves to his clothing like old tepee smoke. He almost choked in the wetness of the clouds. He stumbled, almost fell—

And then, wonderfully, he was floating on a soft green wind that tasted of the earth and the wild things that grew in the earth, and the floating became a gentle drifting down the wind river of dreams . . . .

Ishatai returned to the world of man.

The mark of the Spirit was on him, plain for all to see.

The People knew. There was an ancient wisdom in them, a knowledge that hinted of half-forgotten words and half-remembered places, a wisdom that whispered of dark and fearful things, and of the way the wizards danced when the world was born. In the shadows of the tepees and around the fires that were orange in the night, The People spoke of Ishatai. They watched him with dark staring eyes that were almost afraid to hope again. They waited for him to speak fully of the words that he alone had heard.

Ishatai waited, waited for the sign.

For months, there was nothing.

Then, quite suddenly and without warning, the sign was given to him. A small black cloud drifted across the face of the sun and out of the cloud, miraculously, an eagle flew. The eagle spread his great wings against the sky and swooped down straight at the tepees of The People, his talons taut and extended.

The eagle screamed.

The eagle checked his dive at the last possible moment and skimmed up over the tops of the cottonwood trees. Just as the eagle vanished, there was a crash of thunder that rolled and echoed in the blue sky.

The Spirit had spoken.

That same night, Ishatai stood in the silver light of the Mother Moon and told The People of his journey above the clouds. The words of the Spirit were liquid on his tongue.

The People listened: children with eyes full of wonder, old men whose bones grew cold away from the tepee fires, warriors who gripped their bows and rifles, women who had lost many men. . . .

The People believed.

Before morning, riders slipped away from the reservation. They rode for the Staked Plains and for Mexico and for the land of the Cheyenne. They carried more than a summons, more than a message. They carried hope. There was not a man who rode that night who was not stirred by the same singing vision: *This was our land, this dark land on which I ride. It will be ours again!*

And the power grew and grew in the heart of Ishatai,

Ishatai the strange and lonely one, Ishatai the dreamer. For many great dreams had been given to The People in the endless years since the beginning of time, but the greatest dream of all had been given to Ishatai, and Ishatai was young.

Curtis

Curtis, who had ridden in from Wade with a small escort two days ago, leaned back against his hard chair and stretched out his long legs under the concealing surface of the polished brown table. He was tired and feeling the weight of his forty-seven years, but he was relaxed. He had seen Maria last night and if he could shake loose from Davidson he would see her again tonight.

The news of Ishatai had brought him to Fort Sill for a conference in double-quick time. He had jumped at the chance to come. There was Maria, of course, but she wasn't the whole story. Ishatai meant trouble, and there was always a chance that something useful might come out of the talks. Curtis was more than willing to listen to any sort of reasonable suggestion. The killing of the Indian boy had left a sour taste in his mouth. There had to be a better way of handling things.

Unfortunately, it was already becoming obvious that the meeting would accomplish nothing new. They were just hashing over old ideas and stale policies. It was only early afternoon but Curtis was bored with the fog of pointless talk.

John Davidson, C.O. at Sill, was holding forth at considerable length. He had been talking for what seemed like hours—long, slow hours. Samuel Reed, the Indian agent, was still listening intently. Quaker or not, Sam Reed was getting madder by the minute.

He had had his troubles, Sam Reed. Curtis admired the man and felt sorry for him; to Davidson, the agent was just a damned nuisance. Curtis had talked with Reed a number of times and had some idea of what Reed was up against. Sam Reed was agent for the Comanches, Kiowas, and Kiowa-Apaches, and that in itself was no bed of roses. He was a good man, maybe too good, and whenever he stuck out his hand with an olive branch in it somebody bit it.

Samuel Reed had taken over the agency from his fellow Quakers, Lawrie Tatum and James Haworth. The experience of his predecessors had not daunted him. The Friends believed that there was only one way to solve what they thought of as the Indian problem, and that was by understanding and love. The Indians, they felt, had to be protected and helped along the road to civilization. It was a nice idea, but Sam Reed was finding out that it was one thing to crusade for the Noble Red Man at a safe distance and quite another thing to deal with the Comanches in the all too solid flesh.

Curtis listened to the drone of Davidson's voice with half an ear. From where he sat, he could look out through the window while still seeming attentive. He could see across the parade ground to the gray limestone houses of Officers' Row. The last house at the south end of the line was the one that had been occupied by the same admirable captain throughout the entire history of Fort Sill. The captain had become something of a legend in posts all over the frontier. Sill was like any other army post in that officers had the right to choose their quarters according to their rank; whenever a new officer was assigned, he had his pick of the available housing occupied by any officer of lower rank than himself. There were some lieutenants who had to move so often that their wives didn't even bother to unpack their trunks. The inspired captain, who was the junior captain at Sill, had solved this problem very neatly. There was an artesian spring in the cellar of his house. He had gotten the quartermaster to cap the spring, putting in a drain pipe to get rid of the water. Whenever the captain discovered that a new ranking officer was due at Sill, he simply uncapped the spring and flooded his basement. He would then escort the incoming officer through his home, shaking his head sadly. "A nice house, sir, it really is," he would say. "But I have to tell you, it *is* a little damp."

Davidson's voice buzzed on. Curtis forced himself to listen.

"Ishatai!" Davidson snorted. "Do you know what the damned name means, so help me God? Ishatai means Coyote Dung in Comanche. Think of that, gentlemen! Coyote Dung the Messiah. The Indians have gone mad. If they will follow a man named Coyote Dung, they will do anything!"

Curtis nodded to show that he was listening.

"We're in for trouble," Davidson said for about the tenth time. "*Real* trouble. The Comanches are coming into the reservation by the barrel, and it's not the agency beef that's bringing them—nor the fine words of Mr. Reed here either. The Kiowas are all stirred up. I've even seen some Cheyennes snooping around. By heaven, Kicking Bird tells me that the Comanches are actually going to put on a Sun Dance, and after *that* anything can happen. It isn't enough that they run off my horses and mules from my own corral, oh no. I'm telling you, they're going to use this reservation—this protected sanctuary we've handed to them—to terrorize every blasted settlement between here and the Rio Grande."

"That's what they've always used it for," Curtis said mildly.

Davidson slammed his desk with his fist. "I don't propose to stand for it, I'll tell you that!"

"Ishatai has harmed no living soul," Samuel Reed said, holding himself in check with an effort. "You can't put a man in prison for having a dream. It would be the end of everything we have tried to do here."

Curtis leaned forward. Maybe Reed did have some ideas. If there was any alternative to the old game of slaughter and counter-slaughter, he wanted to hear it. If only the man would *say* something! Something reasonable, something new—

"Mr. Reed. I ask you in all sincerity for your honest opinion. I am not mocking your ideals. We should be able to talk this thing over without rancor. I am certain that Colonel Davidson agrees with this."

"Certainly, certainly," Davidson said.

"I put it to you, Mr. Reed. What do you think we should do now, in this specific situation? You know full well that the Indians will go out after the Sun Dance. They will be all steamed up and looking for trouble. People are going to get hurt. I know that you do not countenance the murder of civilians, whatever your opinion of the military may be. I ask you, sir. If you have a solution, I for one am ready to listen to it."

Reed looked away. "I will talk to the Indians," he said softly. "I will tell them of the word of God."

"And if they don't listen? They haven't listened yet."

"They *must* listen. If we treat them with honesty and kindness, if we remember the wrongs that we have done to them. . . ."

It was no use. Curtis was disappointed, but he could not go on listening to what Reed said. Whatever the worth of the man's ideals, he had no way of translating them into action. Sam Reed had no plan for holding the Indians in check—indeed, he had no plan at all. There would be no help from him.

Curtis knew what the Sun Dance would mean. It was only common sense that the Sun Dance should be stopped. But he could not prevent it, and neither could Davidson. The army had no authority to act on the reservation unless Reed requested it. If the army moved in now, there would be hell to pay. Curtis could imagine the speeches in Congress, the editorials in the distant newspapers. The army would be pictured as a gang of bloodthirsty butchers riding roughshod over the helpless Children of Nature. It was not enough, they would say, that the white man had robbed the Indian of his land—now he would rob him of his religion as well. . . .

Ah, the hell with it. It was true and it was false and there wasn't any answer to it. Curtis hated the futility of his position. What choice did he have? For that matter, what choice did the Indians have? They were all actors in an ancient play, and all the lines had been written before they were born. The whole thing—farce, tragedy, comedy, whatever it was—was inevitable. Nothing could be changed.

It was all there, waiting for them. All they could do was to play their parts.

He had his orders. He knew his lines. But, God above, what was a mind for? If only a man could do something, break out, take control—

Curtis reached for his pipe, thankful that the meeting was nearly over. He looked forward without enthusiasm to another evening in Davidson's company. It would be hours before he could get away from him.

He would have liked to have been able to walk through the reservation, taking a look at the Indians he would soon have to hunt down. That was out of the question, though. Davidson wouldn't like it, and neither would Reed. It would just stir up trouble ahead of time. And the Indians he wanted to see, whoever they were, wouldn't want to talk to him. What could they possibly say to one another? In a sense, he thought, that was the crux of the whole matter. Each side had a position that was wholly logical and self-contained, each on its own terms. There was no way to bridge the gap. The ideas that were needed, and the words to express those ideas, did not exist. The two sides could only collide with each other. They could not interact.

Those were the facts. Honor could not change the facts. Duty could not change the facts. Good will could not change the facts. In time, perhaps, the facts would change. But they would not change soon enough for the Indians, or for Davidson, or for Reed, or for himself.

There would be a fight. It would be senseless in some ways, necessary in others. There would be other fights.

Well, there was Maria. She would be waiting.

He could think of her, and the time would pass.

It was after midnight when he reached the unpainted shack that squatted like a gray growth under the starry vault of the sky. There were no lights.

He knocked gently on the thin wooden door. Maria was not a heavy sleeper. She would hear him. There was no sound from inside. Curtis hesitated. She might have decided that he was not coming. There might be another man in there with her. She had other men, of course.

He knocked again, more loudly this time.

The lamp was lit. Yellow light filtered out weakly through the dirty window.

"*Quién es?*" Her voice, sleepy and familiar. A little bored, perhaps.

His mouth almost touched the scarred wooden door. "It's me. Are you alone?"

"Who is me?" She was playful now.

"Curtis. Are you alone?"

She did not answer him directly. He heard her fumbling with the bolt on the door. The door opened and light poured out.

He slipped inside, quickly. The room was warm with her presence. She closed and locked the door behind him.

"You are late," she said, smiling. Her English was very good when she chose to use it. "I thought you were not coming. You are tired, this night?"

"A little. It does not matter." He looked at her, his gray eyes softening. Her long black hair tumbled over her bare shoulders. Her skin in the lamplight shone like gold. There was still sleep in her large dark eyes. The warm, clean smell of her filled the room.

He took her in his arms and kissed her hair. She drew away from him, gently, and got a bottle and two glasses from the shelf. He crossed to the little table and sat down. Maria took a chair opposite him. Curtis poured out two fairly formidable glasses of whiskey and handed one to her.

"*Salud,*" he said.

Maria smiled sleepily and sipped her drink. She was perfectly natural in her nakedness. Curtis felt more at ease with her than he had ever felt with Helen. There was no need for them to talk. They sat together in friendly silence, enjoying each other.

He drank two glasses of whiskey. She drank most of her glass and then gave the rest to him.

She stood up. "It is late," she said. "In the morning, you will regret the whiskey. Come to bed."

She turned down the wick and blew out the lamp. He undressed quickly and went to her.

She did not hurry him. She pressed her body to his and stroked him with her cool fingers. She held him off when he was ready, kissing his throat. Her hair smelled of the gardenias that grew wild in Mexico. She dug her nails into his back, pulling him down. Her breath was heated in his ear—

They came together savagely, urgently.

When it was over, he was drained, empty. There was no more pain. There were no shadows. There was nothing but a kind of peace. The fires were gone.

She turned away from him and went quickly to sleep. She snored a little.

Curtis got up and lit the lamp. He dressed and left her money on the table by the bottle. He blew out the light again.

He fixed the bolt so it would catch. He stepped outside and closed the door behind him.

He walked away, enjoying the silence of the night and the faint sparks of the morning stars above him. He could feel the peace within him like a tangible thing.

He walked slowly back toward the fort, a tall solitary figure, dark against the lightening sky.

Fox Claw

The tribe was gathering.

Fox Claw watched them come with cold black eyes, eyes that were as steady and unchanging as the rocks of the Shining Mountains. He was very thin, and he knew that it was more than food that he needed. There was a lack in him or around him, an emptiness, as though some vital strand had been cut from the fabric of his life. He was all skin and bones and long ropelike muscles, a tall gaunt skeleton of a man the gods seemed to be creating for purposes of their own. There were great dark hollows beneath the jutting cheekbones of his face; the face was strangely unfinished, a face roughed out of unyielding stone by forces that had no time to spare. It was a face that had been hardened into a shape that was set and final, and yet there was something about it that seemed unformed. It was not yet complete. There were other details of that face, hidden and latent, waiting for some other time or some other place to come into being.

Buffalo Tongue, who had called him father, was dead. He was certain that the boy had seen the buffalo on Spirit Hill, just as Fox Claw had seen him there many years before. For that, he was glad. It was a link between them. Buffalo Tongue had hunted the buffalo in his short life. He had stolen horses and known women. That was as it should be. That was good. He had died in battle without becoming old and useless. That, too, might be good.

Fox Claw missed the boy. He knew that he had lost something he could never have again. A son, yes, but more than a son. He had lost a piece of his life; the web that reached from the present to the past was broken. There would be no more boys like Buffalo Tongue. The new ones would be—different.

He would remember him, and the way that he had died.

Fox Claw had heard the words of Ishatai. They had been long in coming, but they had come. He had listened carefully, and he had willed himself to believe that the words were the words of the Spirit. He could not believe, and that was all. He had felt nothing, not even disappointment. The words were just the words of Ishatai. Fox Claw had had some experience with bullets, and he suspected that they could kill Ishatai as easily as they had killed Buffalo Tongue. As for the dead warriors coming back again—well, the talk of Ishatai was big talk. Fox Claw had seen no dead warriors riding into the reservation.

Still, many of The People had believed in the words of the prophet and that was good. It was because of the words of Ishatai that the tribe was gathering. Never before had Fox Claw seen such a thing. The memories of the oldest men could recall nothing like it. Every day and every night The People came in. Some of them came alone. Others came in groups of twenty or even thirty men and women and children. Fox Claw did not know them all: Yamparikas and Kotsotekas and Nokonis and nameless ones, all the scattered bands of the Comanches. The entire tribe was not there, of course; that was unthinkable. But The People were many. Their strength was greater than it had ever been. Some of the Kwahadis were camped on the reservation, although he had not seen Broken Bow. All of the great war leaders were in: Quanah and Wild Horse and Shaking Hand. The Kiowas were in. Some of the Cheyennes had come.

There were many fires burning on the reservation.

Fox Claw was ready. He had only to wait until the others were also ready.

Fox Claw had seen the Sun Dance of the Kiowas, but he had never taken part in one. The Sun Dance was not a custom of the Comanches, although many tribes had it. It was said that the Sun Dance made power for the whole tribe that put it on. If many tribes had made use of it, Fox Claw reasoned, including some that were distant in the northern plains, then it must be powerful medicine. It was said that it took an entire tribe to stage a Sun Dance, but even a part of the Comanche tribe was larger than many tribes that Fox Claw knew.

By the first day of June, when the oaks and willows and cottonwoods and elms were green and full, the reservation was surging with activity. The days were suddenly not long enough for everything that had to be done. A pulsing rhythm of life flowed through the clustered tepees like a river of magic. It was impossible not to be caught up in it, not to hope. There was a vibrance in the very air, as though life itself had become a kind of dance.

One day, before the beginning of the true Sun Dance, a group of warriors rode down to Elk Creek and built a circular fence out of logs. The warriors went about their task with great solemnity. This was play, but it was a new kind of play. The fence was designed to represent an enemy outpost, and everyone knew who the enemy was. Stockaded villages were not the Indian way.

This was a fort of the buffalo hunters.

Every warrior on the reservation took part in a furious charge at the rail fence, scattering the logs with their anger. The women and children trailed along with them, shouting encouragement. Fox Claw rode Watcher in the attack, striking with his lance as he had struck the real camp of the buffalo hunters not many months ago. It was more than play; it was pantomime. Fox Claw was in dead earnest in the charge. His heart swelled within him. Now, at last, there would be a dance of victory. He could tell how he had counted coup, and The People would know that it had been no rail fence that he had charged. The People would listen to him.

There were other days, and other nights. In some ways, it was the richest time of Fox Claw's life. It had not been easy for him to stand alone, although there had been no other possible choice for him. It meant much to him to be supported in all his actions by The People. It was good to be a part of something greater than himself.

When the Sun Dance finally started, it was a gradual thing, slow and sedate. It may have been, Fox Claw thought, that it did not begin at all. It simply flowed by barely perceptible stages until it was *there*.

A crier rode through the massed tepees, calling out that it was time. Just as the colors left the earth and the shadows fell, The People gathered in a great crowd at the Sun Dance lodge. They stood in a large circle just outside the eastern opening. They were quiet and orderly, subdued by their numbers. They were awed by their own strength.

There was no command, no signal. Everyone knew that it was time to dance. The dancing began.

All night The People danced. It was a slow dance, without frenzy or fury. The dancers hardly seemed to move at all. There was no sound except for the soft shuffling of moccasins on earth and the crackling of the fires. Fox Claw had never heard such silence from so many people. They were still waiting, still making themselves ready.

They danced through the white light of dawn. The morning came, the sun lifted into the sky. The light of the sun lanced through the doorway of the lodge—

The Drum started.

A mighty Drum it was, a huge round Drum inside the lodge of the Sun Dance. It took six drummers to beat on that Drum. The lodge trembled with its quick beat. Sweat poured from the bodies of the drummers and smeared the paint on their faces. The brush walls of the lodge caught the sound and magnified it. The drumming became a vast heartbeat of the earth itself.

The dancers moved more quickly now, matching their steps to the insistent beat. Rattles took up the rhythm. The women began to sway, chanting a shrill chorus that heightened the beat of the Drum. The bursts of sound shook the morning air.

The dance was wilder, faster. The smell of sweat mixed with the smoke from the fires. The flames leaped higher.

The warriors moved into the lodge. First one and then another would dance through the lodge door and perform with jerky hopping movements, their eyes fixed on the notch of the forked center pole. They clamped eagle-bone whistles between their teeth and they blew short piercing screams on the whistles as they danced. The noise inside the lodge was deafening.

Above the heads of the whirling dancers, the grass-stuffed buffalo watched with eyes that shone like living fire.

The Drum pounded on: calling, urging, demanding.

The dance was life; it could not stop. The Drum was the rhythm of life; none could remember when it had not sounded. The People danced until they dropped. They crawled away to sleep and eat, and then they came back to dance again.

Ishatai was always there. He hurled himself into the dance like a man gone mad. Four times he fainted, and four times he recovered to tell of his visions from the Spirit.

And then, abruptly, it was over.

The Drum stopped.

The incredible silence swept over the encampment like a wind of death.

Ishatai staggered out of the lodge, his face haggard and stained with sweat. He threw up his hands. His hoarse voice was little more than a whisper.

"My brothers," he said. The People strained to hear him, breathing hard. "My brothers, we are strong!"

The People nodded. Ah, they were many, many. . . .

"We will sleep this night, and tomorrow our weapons will be made ready. Tomorrow night we ride!"

Late that night, Fox Claw was roused from a deep sleep by the sound of hoofbeats. He did not wait to puzzle over their meaning. He slipped from his bed and stepped outside.

He could see them clearly in the starlight. Indians, many Indians. He looked closely, shock and despair rising in him like angry smoke. They were Comanches. There were warriors there, but this was no war party. The women were riding out too, many of them with children on their backs.

Fox Claw shivered in the cool night air. He recognized Horse Back of the Nokonis. It was his band, all of them. He ran around in front of the old man's horse, forcing him to stop.

"Get out of the way, my son," the old man said.

Fox Claw hesitated. He crouched . . . .

A strong hand touched his shoulder. He turned. Quanah stood at his side in the darkness, tall and steady as a tree that grows where the water is good. "Let him go. It is the way. We want no warriors with troubled hearts."

Fox Claw sighed and backed away. The Nokonis rode by, shadows in the starlight, saying nothing. The hoofbeats of their ponies died away in the stillness.

"They are not the first to go," said Quanah.

"I feel shame for them."

Quanah shrugged. His calm went so deep that nothing could shake it. "I have ridden with Horse Back in other days. He is a good man."

"Good man! Why does he ride away like a woman?" Fox Claw was hurt and bewildered.

"Perhaps he is wiser than we are," Quanah said quietly.

Fox Claw rubbed his eyes. The night was strangely hushed; the pale tepees were like ghost dwellings around him. He forced his anger from him. He was a warrior. A warrior did not act like a child.

"The plan of Ishatai is a good plan," he said. "I say nothing of the Spirit. We know where the soldiers are expecting us, and we will fool them. We ride to the northwest, across the Canadian. We ride to Adobe Walls, where the buffalo hunters sleep. We have many warriors. It is a good plan."

"The plan is good. As for the rest, who can say?"

Quanah turned and walked away.

Fox Claw went back into his tepee. He knew that there would be no more sleep for him that night. He lay on his bed, eyes wide open, staring at nothing. Somewhere in that great ghost village of the Sun Dance, he knew that Quanah Parker also would not sleep.

Somewhere in that dark encampment, Quanah walked alone.

Adobe Walls

Just after midnight, in the first morning hour of the 27th of June, twenty-eight men and one woman dozed fitfully in the old trading post of Adobe Walls. Several of the men were sleeping in Hanrahan's saloon. William Olds and his wife were in the back of Rath and Wright's store. Most of the men slept outside on the ground, and the two Shadler brothers had bedded down in their wagon.

The night was hot and sultry and flooded with moonlight. Every door in Adobe Walls was wide open. In the still air, the sound of owls hooting in the timber that lined the creek east of the Walls was unnaturally loud and clear.

The men at Adobe Walls had taken no special precautions that night. Once they had moved south of the dead line of the Arkansas they knew that Indian attacks were always a possibility. It was something they lived with, like the weather. Lately, there had been plenty of signs. Within the past week they had learned of two nearby raids. Two hunters, Dudley and Wallace, had been jumped on Chicken Creek. Both had been killed—Wallace by a large wooden stake that had been driven through him, pinning him to the ground. Another hunter had brought in word that two other men had died. Cheyenne Jack, who was English, and Blue Billy, a German, had been killed on a tributary of the Salt Fork of the Red River. The men at the Walls had not actually seen any Indians recently—but they knew they were around.

Every man at Adobe Walls that night slept with one eye open.

The most impressive thing about Adobe Walls was its loneliness. In the clear light of the swollen silver moon, its buildings stood out sharply and distinctly in the middle of nowhere. It was hard to know just what to call Adobe Walls. It was not a fort, despite the stockade around the store belonging to Myers and Leonard and the mess house—a stockade built from cottonwood logs that had been hauled from Reynolds Creek six miles on the other side of the Canadian. It was a kind of trading post, but it was more than that. It was a headquarters for the hide men south of the Arkansas. Most of all, perhaps, it was a sanctuary—a tiny outpost of safety in a wild and difficult land.

Its position heightened its sense of isolation. It stood in the midst of a great meadow, not quite surrounded by low hills. To the southeast was the valley of the Canadian; standing at the Walls, a man could not quite see the river itself, which was several miles distant. The hills to the north and northwest were gentle slopes, but to the east there was a sharper rise. There, partly screened by a growth of willows, cottonwoods, hackberry, and chinaberry trees that lined Walls Creek, a buttelike hill with a definite cap rock jutted above the plain.

There were no buildings of adobe at Adobe Walls. The place took its name from an earlier post, built in 1844 by William Bent to serve as a trading post for the Indians. The post had been abandoned, though traces of it still remained—sections of walls made of adobe brick standing four to five feet high. The present post, located a mile and a half northeast of the ruins, had not been there long. It had been financed by A. C. Myers of Dodge City, who had agreed to set up a supply center and hide market on the Canadian for the buffalo hunters.

In the moonlight, the layout of Adobe Walls was clear and simple. The main buildings all stood in a row, facing east. The south end of the little line was taken up by Rath and Wright's sod-house store, selling general merchandise and managed by James Langton. Next came Hanrahan's well-patronized sod saloon. Then, next to the stockade, was Tom O'Keefe's blacksmith shop, fifteen feet square, set up to repair the wagons. Finally, on the north end of the line, was the stockade. The southwest corner of the stockade was taken up by the long mess house. The northeast corner was the store of Myers and Leonard. Between the mess house and the store there was a well.

That was all there was at Adobe Walls.

At two o'clock in the morning on that hot moonlit night of the 27th of June, a big cottonwood ridge pole in the prairie sod roof of Hanrahan's saloon cracked with a sharp report. Two men, Shepard and Mike Welch, who had been sleeping in the saloon, woke up. It was obvious that the roof might not hold until daylight. Shepard and Welch roused the others. Even the pet crow that belonged to Mrs. Olds woke up and began to squawk. Mrs. Olds got up to calm the crow.

Within ten minutes, nobody was asleep at Adobe Walls except for the two Shadler brothers in their wagon with their big Newfoundland dog.

The men pitched in, with the aid of considerable profanity, to shore up the ridge pole. A party went out to cut a prop behind the stockade. It took a good three hours to get the support in place.

By that time, the sky was reddening in the east. Most of the men went back to bed, but they moved inside the buildings because the night had cooled. Billy Dixon and Jim Hanrahan, who had their wagons already loaded for a hunt they had planned, decided that they might as well stay up and get off to an early start. They sent young Billy Ogg to get the horses. The horses were about a quarter of a mile away, pastured to the southeast along Adobe Walls Creek.

Dixon strolled over near the blacksmith shop where he had been sleeping. He was a stocky, powerful man with a moustache and a slightly receding hairline. His wide-set eyes were restless. The moon was gone and the faint light of dawn was still tricky. He tied up his bedroll and tossed it into the front of his loaded wagon. He checked his saddle horse, picketed to a stake pin near the wagon.

Something made him glance toward the east.

He froze in his tracks. He could not see clearly but he could make out a large number of dark objects moving out of the timber that lined Adobe Walls Creek. The dark figures fanned out in a great arc.

The hazy red sun lifted over the cap rock of the butte.

Before Dixon could act, there was an incredible piercing scream—one high-pitched solid yell of sound that poured from countless throats. Dixon had never heard anything like it. Instantly, he caught the pounding roar of charging horses. The wall of human sound dissolved into the yipping cries of individual warriors.

"Great Godalmighty," breathed Dixon.

At first, there was no time to think. Billy Dixon acted on instinct. In his experience, Indians meant horse thieves. They must be after the horse herd. He grabbed the rope of his plunging horse, tore it out of the stake pin, and tied it to his wagon. That way his horse could not be stampeded with the others.

He reached into the wagon and pulled out his rifle, hoping to get off a shot or two before the Indians broke their charge and ran off with the stock. But he saw at once that the Indians were not going to break. They were coming straight as an arrow for the buildings of Adobe Walls.

"Great Godalmighty," Billy Dixon said again.

Late in his life, when the old free days of the plains were gone forever, Billy Dixon would remember that charge and rejoice that it had been given to him to see it. There had never been anything to match it on the southern plains. There were more Indians in that charge than Billy Dixon had seen in a lifetime on the frontier.

He got off one shot and ran for it. Hanrahan's saloon was the nearest building, so he headed there. The big door was shut fast. He hollered. The men inside yanked open the door to let him in. At that exact moment, Billy Ogg ran through the door and collapsed in exhaustion. It was a miracle that he had made it back alive.

There was no panic. The hunters were up and ready. They knew well enough that they owed their lives to the cottonwood ridge pole that had cracked, disturbing their sleep. If they had all been caught asleep outside—

Well, there was no point in thinking about it.

The hunters at Adobe Walls, most of them still dressed in their underwear, had only a few seconds to brace for the charge. The men found themselves divided into three groups. Eleven hunters were holed up in Myers and Leonard's store at the northeast corner of the stockade. Six men and Mrs. Olds were in Rath and Wright's store on the south end of the line. In Hanrahan's saloon, holding down the center, Billy Dixon had eight men with him: Jim Hanrahan, Bat Masterson, Shepard, Mike Welch, Billy Ogg, Hiram Watson, James McKinley, and Bermuda Carlisle.

There had been no time to warn the two Shadler brothers. Although no one knew it yet, they were still in their wagon.

The mass of Indians never wavered. They pressed home their charge with a crazy courage. The morning air erupted with an explosion of shouts, bullets, and arrows. It seemed for a moment that they would ride right through the buildings, but the buildings were solid and they held against the shock of the horsemen. The Indians surrounded the post and poured in a withering fire. Every window shattered. Some of the Indians dismounted and hammered on the doors with their rifle butts.

If the hunters thought of the odds or of their chances for survival, they never showed it. Most of them were armed with the Sharps Big Fifty buffalo rifles and they opened up with cool, steady deliberation. They were the best marksmen on the frontier and they showed it. A man like Billy Dixon who could drop two hundred buffalo in a single day without missing a shot found the Indians easy pickings.

The acrid smell of gunsmoke inside the buildings brought tears to the eyes. The barrels of the Big Fifties got so hot they burned the hands. The hunters threw up a wall of fire around their buildings, and they selected their targets as calmly as though they were shooting buffalo.

Nothing could stand against those twenty-six guns.

The Indians fell in heaps, shot to pieces by the big slugs. They began to withdraw. Many of them risked their lives to carry off dead or wounded warriors.

Within an hour the post itself was clear. The Indians had pulled back to attempt a duel at long-range. It was a fatal mistake. The Sharps Big Fifties had the range on them, and the marksmanship of the hunters was fantastic.

Billy Dixon estimated that there had been seven hundred warriors in that first charge. Probably, his guess was too high. But it had been a formidable force. Except for the two Shadler brothers, overwhelmed in their wagon with their dog, the hunters at Adobe Walls had not lost a man.

Briefly, the luck of the hunters deserted them. Billy Tyler left his cover and stepped out into the stockade to get a better shot. A bullet caught him in the lungs before he could fire.

A strange sound carried over the grassy clearing that held the thin row of buildings that was Adobe Walls. It was the call of a bugle, expertly played. For a moment the hunters thought that the army had arrived, but they soon realized that the bugle was blown by an Indian. He knew all the proper calls. That suited the men at the Walls just fine, for they knew the calls, too. When the Indian bugler sounded the second charge, they were ready and waiting.

The charge was shattered almost before it could begin.

In Hanrahan's saloon, there was plenty of whiskey but not much ammunition. Billy Dixon and Jim Hanrahan decided to go get some before the next charge hit. They threw open the big door of the saloon and lit out for Rath and Wright's. Bullets buzzed by them like bees, but they made it untouched.

There were only six men in Rath and Wright's, and they were worried about Mrs. Olds. Dixon decided to stay and add his rifle to the defense of the south end of the line. Jim Hanrahan loaded a sack with cartridges and sprinted for the saloon. He drew a furious hail of fire but he got there safely.

By two o'clock that afternoon, the firing was sporadic. The Indians had pulled back to the hills. Most of them were to the east, on the bluff, but some were scattered in the low hills to the northwest.

By four, the shooting stopped entirely.

The men of Adobe Walls, sure of their position, stepped out to look around.

It was a startling sight. Billy Dixon never forgot it. In some ways, it was hard to believe that there had been a battle. The sun was hot on the grassy meadow and the still air was filled with black gnats. The birds, frightened away by the crash of gunfire, had come back in some numbers. Billy could hear larks and doves clearly. The wild flowers were everywhere: thistles with a lavender flower, yellow blossoms with black center cones, deep red delicate flowers showing through the tall grass.

In other ways, the result of the fight were plain to see. The grass was stained with large patches of drying blood. Fifty-six dead horses littered the field. No man knew how many dead and wounded Indians had been carried off with the Indians in their retreat, but there were still thirteen dead Indians sprawled where they had fallen. Billy found the last one himself. It was a Comanche warrior seated in a very natural position just to the west of Rath and Wright's store. He was sitting with his legs crossed, his head turned to one side. A bullet had broken his neck. His feathered lance was stuck into the ground; Billy had fired at it twice from the store without knowing what it was. He picked it up for a souvenir.

Before they went back to their posts for the night, the hunters buried the Shadler brothers and Billy Tyler in one unmarked grave near the north side of the corral.

The night was quiet; there was no shooting.

The next day the stench from the field was terrific. There were some scattered shots from the bluff to the east, but the Indians were too far away to hit anything with their weapons. The crow belonging to Mrs. Olds flew from one horse carcass to another, screeching. The hunters went out and worked for hours in the hot sun, pushing the dead horses and Indians onto buffalo hides. They attached ropes to the hides and pulled them by hand away from the buildings; they had no horses left. They tossed some dirt over some of them, and others they just left to rot on the prairie.

The night was hot with a fading moon. Again, there was no shooting but no one could sleep. They could hear the owls hooting to the east, and they knew that some of those owls were Comanches. The men at Adobe Walls had won every fight, but they were not out of the woods yet. They were twenty-five men in the middle of nowhere and they were surrounded by the largest force of Indians ever assembled on the southern plains.

On the afternoon of the third day, the Indians made another fatal mistake. A small party of them showed themselves on top of the bluff east of the Walls. One of them was painted yellow. Another, probably a Cheyenne, had a magnificent feather headdress.

Bat Masterson grinned at Billy Dixon. "There's a shot for you," he said.

Billy squinted. "Too far," he said.

The other hunters egged him on. Billy had a reputation as a marksman.

Billy shrugged. "Close on to a mile," he said. His guess was pretty close. The range was 1,538 yards.

"Bet a dollar," Bat said.

Billy held out his hand and someone gave him a Big Fifty. He had lost his own crossing the Canadian, and had used a .44 Sharps through most of the fight.

He adjusted the sights. He rested the heavy gun on the sill of a window. He took aim twice.

Billy fired. For a moment he thought he had missed. His target was so far away that the crash of the Big Fifty had died away before there was any movement on the bluff.

Every eye was fixed on the cap rock of that rust-colored hill.

When it happened, it happened quickly. The warrior in the feathered headdress twisted out of his saddle and fell.

"Well, I'll be damned," said Billy Dixon.

Fox Claw

At the moment of Billy Dixon's shot, Fox Claw was mounted on Watcher on the bluff east of Adobe Walls. His eyes burned like hot coals in his skull. Ishatai, naked except for a breechclout, was covered with yellow paint. The prophet sat on his white horse, watching the ruin of his dreams. Fox Claw did not look at him; Ishatai no longer mattered. The Cheyenne with the splendid war bonnet was still urging Ishatai to try to get the warriors together for another charge.

When the Cheyenne fell from his saddle they all knew that there was no hope left. It was a sign no man could mistake. Ishatai hung his head and moaned like an animal in pain.

It was then, at the worst possible time, when the Cheyenne was still sprawled on the rocks and the Indians were in a state of shock from Billy Dixon's unbelievable shot, that they heard the bugle.

The Indians had no bugler now.

The soldiers were coming.

Ishatai wheeled and galloped off the ridge. The Indian warriors ran for their horses. They were utterly demoralized. There was no plan, no thought, no strategy. It was every man for himself in a blind rout.

Fox Claw could hear the cheering from Adobe Walls.

He smiled a tired, bitter smile. He took his time. He tied his rifle to his saddle and slipped out his lance. Framed against the afternoon sky, looking into the setting sun, he lifted his lance high above his head.

He was ready to die. But he was not going to die like a rabbit in flight. He felt shame for The People, running away before the attack had even started. There was a better way to die.

Dies Young rode up the bluff to his side. A grin split his ugly face. He said nothing.

Three other warriors joined them, two Comanches and a Kiowa.

That was all.

"Let us give the soldiers something to remember," Fox Claw said.

He turned Watcher toward the sound of the bugles.

Curtis

Curtis had set his trap with care.

He had not, of course, deliberately baited his trap with the hunters at Adobe Walls. Still, the Indians had attacked the trading post; he could not alter that fact. He was prepared to exploit the situation to his utmost.

He had hoped that the Indians would stand and fight. He knew he could handle them. He wanted a clean, decisive battle to wipe out the stain of his killing of the Comanche boy, Buffalo Tongue. If he could catch the Indians massed in one place he could destroy them with honor.

But Curtis was a practical man. Jim, his Tonk scout, had explained the position succinctly. "They ride away plenty damn fast," Jim had said. Very well. If he could not have the fight he wanted he would have a slaughter.

He had over two hundred men with him, divided into four companies. As he saw it, the choices open to the fleeing Indians were limited. They could head north from Adobe Walls, toward the Arkansas. If they did, he and Davidson would have plenty of time to cut off their return to the reservation. They might ride west, toward Taos. They might go south, toward the Staked Plains. They might ride to the east, toward Fort Sill and the reservation.

Curtis took his time getting into position. He knew from the sound of the firing that the men at Adobe Walls were not in any immediate danger. If the Indians had failed in their first attack, the big guns at the Walls could hold them off indefinitely.

He stationed two companies of cavalry—his own A Company and C Company under Captain Taylor—just to the south of Adobe Walls, on the Walls side of the Canadian. He sent B Company around behind the bluff to the east of the trading post. Company E was flanked an equal distance to the west.

Captain Taylor, with his company at full strength, was to stand as a ready mobile reserve. Company C was not to charge. Their job was to sit tight. If any outfit got into trouble, a bugle call would bring Captain Taylor into the fight with sixty fresh troopers. If by some miracle they *all* got into deep water, Adobe Walls was available as a position of strength. They could hold out there until hell froze solid.

There were no bugle calls until every man was where he should be. Then Curtis dropped his right hand sharply. Trooper Maxwell, the trumpeter of A Company, sounded the charge.

The army thundered forward under the blue afternoon skies.

The charge was a tonic to him. It was all the power and excitement and glory of the army wrapped up in one solid roar of movement. There were no doubts in a charge. The guidons snapped and the standards were bluer than the sky, their eagles screaming in the wind. Sabers flashed in the sun. The big troop horses bowed their necks and hurtled forward like juggernauts.

It was raw power, magnificently controlled.

The straight blue lines converged on Adobe Walls.

Curtis narrowed his gray eyes against the wind. He saw no Indians ahead of him. They must be breaking the other way—

Then he saw them.

Five Indian horsemen topped a low rise so suddenly that they might almost have been dropped to the earth by an invisible hand. They came at a full gallop straight at the charging cavalry. Five men! It was incredible. There was no time to think.

The men of A Company reacted with a speed that did them credit. There was a ragged volley from the ready Springfields. Two of the Indians went down, shot out of their saddles. Curtis switched his saber to his left hand, the hand that held the reins, and snatched out his Colt .45 with his right. He threw down on a painted warrior who couldn't have been thirty yards away when he pulled the trigger. The Comanche pitched from his horse. The horse reared and was hit the next instant.

The two Indians that were left came on in their crazy charge. He could see them clearly; they etched themselves into his eyes in the second before they struck. One was tall and thin with a lance cradled against his arm; he sat straight on his horse as though daring the soldiers to shoot him down. The other was a heavier man, and he was the most astonishing rider Curtis had ever seen. He was all over his horse, presenting no target at all.

They hit the cavalry line with an audible crash. It was beautifully done, magnificently executed. In a split second one trooper was speared from his horse by the lance, and another was knocked sprawling by a terrific blow from a war club. The two Indians were through the line before A Company could even pause in its charge; they hightailed it at a full gallop, riding at an angle that would miss the soldiers held back in reserve.

Curtis swore, but he did not make the mistake of going after them. He knew that C Company wouldn't break ranks to pursue the two Indians; he would court-martial the lot of them, including Taylor, if they abandoned the battle plan without orders. If he spun A Company around he would ruin everything. He had the main body of Indians caught in a pincers. He was not going to be diverted by two Comanche madmen.

He gave a hand signal to Trooper Maxwell. Maxwell was still at his side where he belonged; Curtis was pleased that discipline had held.

The trumpeter sounded the charge again. The quick notes of the bugle cut through the dust and confusion like a knife.

The line straightened.

Company A of the Twelfth roared back to the attack.

It was not a fight. It was a massacre. Company A hit the disorganized Indians like a sledgehammer. The Indians were already engaged by B Company in a holding action; they could not begin to handle the onslaught of Curtis and his men.

The army became a killing machine.

Curtis enjoyed it while it lasted. His men knew what to do and they did it. The Springfields and Colts blasted away until the acrid gunsmoke was heavy in the afternoon air. The big cavalry sabers finished the job.

The army took no prisoners that warm June day at Adobe Walls.

Some of the Indians got away. It was impossible to contain them all. But they had been hurt. It wasn't likely that they could ever get together such a big force again. They had been thoroughly licked.

Curtis had done his job well.

Ishatai

Ishatai got back alive from Adobe Walls. He turned his broken white horse out to graze; there was plenty of grass now for all the horses that were left. He washed the dirty yellow paint from his numb body. He went and looked at the deserted Sun Dance lodge, but he did not stay long. He walked to his empty tepee and sat before it, staring at nothing.

The moon was cold that night, waning and lonely in a sea of pitiless stars. A soft wind whispered a song of sadness through the cottonwood trees. It was a gentle song, a healing song, as though the wind were trying to ease the hurts that were too much for a man to bear. Ishatai was thankful for the wind, but it was only the wind. It was not enough.

The night was filled with tears.

He was alone again, terribly alone. He had spent

most of his life alone, but it was harder now. He listened to the owls calling in dark liquid voices down by the creek. Many a night, when he was a boy, he had sat out under the stars like this and talked with the owls. He could not bring himself to speak to them tonight.

His eyes closed on emptiness. The dream was dead.

For Ishatai, there would be no more dreams, forever.

PART TWO

The Hunt
1874–75

Fox Claw

The buffalo were called by an ancient rhythm, a restless pulse that stirred through a reborn earth as insistently as it had in the first green springtime of the world. The small scattered bunches that stained the windswept winter plains were drawn closer to each other. They united and formed great bellowing herds that flattened the fresh new grass. The herds no longer stretched like a dark flowing sea from horizon to horizon, but they were still large. The glossy red-brown calves ran with delight on their uncertain legs. The big bulls pawed bare patches in the dirt. They fought their age-old fights, colliding with impacts that sent shudders through the clouds of yellow dust. The cows watched them with seeming unconcern, waiting.

Slowly, the great herds shifted toward the north. They did not move far, perhaps two hundred miles during the whole of the hot summer months. But they did move, ponderously, pushed by the growing glare of the sun. Summer had come again to the Staked Plains.

Fox Claw did not mind the heat, though water was scarce and hard to find. The sun burned into his shoulders and the dry heat warmed his bones. It was pleasant to lie on his belly against the warmth of the earth and to dip his face into the waterhole to drink. It was good to be able to watch the lazy white butterflies that rode the hot updrafts of the air. It was good to see the violent dust devils chasing each other under the hard blue sky.

At night, the Staked Plains changed. The gentle night winds were cool and alive, alive with friendly whispers and familiar smells. The desert smells were sharper at night. The winds brought the scent of cooling sands and white stones and rich greasewood. The stars choked the velvet sky and they were so big and clear that he could see the different colors in them: cold silver and warm red and iced blue. The glow of the desert moon filled the world with a steady light of wonder.

Surely, this was a land apart—a land of light-reflecting sands and scorching sun and racing cloud shadows that hurried along through shimmering waves of heat. It was a place to refuge precisely because it was a hard land. Broken Bow was too old to dream, and too wise; he had not ridden to Adobe Walls. His small band was almost intact. Sometimes, dozing in the rare and shifting shade, Fox Claw could come close to believing that Adobe Walls had never happened.

One of the camp dogs gave birth to a litter of tiny black and white puppies. Three of the puppies lived. They screwed open their wet little eyes and staggered around the camp, somehow surviving the games the children played with them. In the violet evenings, after they had gorged themselves on their emaciated and long-suffering mother, the pups would be invigorated by the cooling air. They would try out their clumsy legs, running impossible races through the brown grass.

It had been many years since Fox Claw had a dog of his own, and for a time he did not admit to himself that he had one now. But one of the pups, a lively male with two white circles around his liquid eyes that made him look like an owl, spent an increasing amount of time in his company. He chewed on his moccasins with a comfortable pride of ownership and sometimes at night he would sidle over and stick his cold black nose against Fox Claw's cheek. Fox Claw began to save scraps for the puppy to eat, and one day he gave the dog a name.

He called him Little Cousin. He liked the name. If the wolf was Coyote's brother, it was also true that the dog was the cousin of Coyote. That was one reason why dog meat had always been forbidden to The People.

Fox Claw was absurdly fond of the dog. He knew that he was being foolish about Little Cousin, but that did not change his feelings. He had seen it happen with other men. In a tepee without children, it was said, a dog could become a tyrant. Childless men had been known to carry their dogs on their saddles so their feet would not get tired.

They made quite a pair. As the weeks of summer slipped by, the puppy got fatter and fatter until his stubby legs could hardly support the weight of his body. Fox Claw remained as lean as ever, a tall skeleton that had somehow acquired a thin covering of scarred bronzed skin and whipcord muscles. The contrast gave Fox Claw an obscure pleasure. The fatter Little Cousin got the more it pleased him. He laughed and talked to the dog as he would have talked to a child. "You are getting too heavy to lift," he would say, taking the pup up in his hard hands. "You are as fat as an old woman. What kind of a warrior will you turn out to be?"

It was good to laugh again.

It was good to be alive.

The hot sun burned into the hard brown land day after day. The dusty blue-green tangles of tumbleweeds scratched across the plains, stopping to rest when the hot winds died. The spikes of the yucca stabbed at the pale blue sky. Slowly the buffalo drifted toward the north. Soon they would be gone until fall.

It was time for the hunt.

The warriors of Broken Bow's band set out in the early dawn, when dampness sparkled in the brown grass of the Staked Plains and the sun was sending up pink streamers from below the distant horizon. They had only twenty hunters; they were small and lost under the bowl of the morning sky.

They found the herd when the white sun was high in the sky. The buffalo were grazing quietly, slowed by the massive heat of the day. The hunters moved up silently against the soft drying wind, smelling the buffalo. They did not speak.

Fox Claw knew that the weak eyes of the buffalo could not see him. His thin hand rested lightly in Watcher's mane. He drank in the sight of the buffalo, trying to imprint it forever on his mind. He looked at the young spike bulls and the great old bulls that weighed a ton and more. He studied the cows, selecting the ones that would yield the best meat. He saw the fat brown calves, playing even in the hammering blaze of the sun. How eternal it all seemed, how changeless out there in the grass under the big sky! And yet he remembered the mighty herds of his childhood, he remembered. . . .

Broken Bow gave the signal.

The warriors charged into the hot wind, their horses drumming on the brown baked earth. They charged in a straight line; they did not have enough men to make an effective surround of the herd.

Fox Claw bared his white teeth. The wind burned his naked body. Dies Young rode bareback, holding on with his knees, but Fox Claw had tied a rope around Watcher and rode with his knees clamped under the rope. His bow was ready in his hands.

The buffalo were very stupid, as always. They kept on grazing until the hunters were almost on top of them. Then they reacted slowly, almost reluctantly. The bulls made a sluggish attempt to form a barrier between the warriors and the cows and calves but they were too late. They bellowed and pawed the hot earth and tossed their sharp white horns.

Fox Claw rode Watcher through the wavering line of bulls. Watcher knew what to do. He picked out a cow and drew up beside her. Fox Claw bent his bow and loosed his arrow in one fluid motion, aiming for the low heart behind the short rib. He drove the feathered arrow completely into the cow; only the feathers showed. With the sudden sound of the released sinew bowstring, Watcher swerved instantly to avoid the charge of the wounded animal.

It was a wild time, a seething melee of heat and shouting hunters and pounding hooves and choking gritty dust. But there was a method in it too, an automatic organization that was built into the very flesh and bones of the warriors and their horses. Watcher wheeled and galloped from cow to cow, and Fox Claw loosed his arrows with deadly precision. By the time the herd was in full flight he had dropped four cows and a bull.

The yellow dust clouds settled slowly. There were seventy dead buffalo sprawled in the blood-stained dirt.

It had been a good hunt.

There would be meat and skins for a long time to come.

The hunters worked quickly. The buffalo had to be skinned and butchered rapidly. They had used no guns, but the roaring of the buffalo had been loud and the pillars of dust could be seen for miles in that flat land.

Fox Claw searched out his arrows. He took his sharp metal knife and left Watcher to stand as a sentinel while he worked. Watcher was trained to flick both of his ears forward if a strange man appeared, and he had never failed Fox Claw in this. He was a horse well named.

It was late when the hunters started back to camp. It always took longer to skin and butcher the buffalo than to kill them. All of the meat was piled in the hides, and the heavy hides were fastened to the backs of the pack horses. The first pale stars dusted the sky. The wind turned fresh and cool.

Fox Claw turned and looked back once.

There was nothing to see in the gathering gloom. Where the buffalo had been there was only the emptiness of the night-shadowed land, and the stars that looked down with blind eyes out of the night.

The next day, while the hunters rested, the women went to work. They sliced the meat into strips and hung the ribbons of dark flesh on the drying racks in the searing sun. They pegged out the stiffening hides, keeping the flesh sides up, and all day long they scraped away the bits of fat and meat.

That night there was a feast. There was dripping sizzling buffalo meat and there was water. That was all—but what else could there be that would add to such a meal? Rich tangy fresh buffalo steaks and clean water to wash them down; anything else would have detracted from it. It gave a man strength and contentment. It was the only proper food. A man could not get sick from eating buffalo meat.

When Fox Claw could eat no more, and the skin of his belly was as taut and swollen as a drum, he sat and smoked with Dies Young. Neither man spoke. It was a night to be shared in silence.

He slept where he was, out under the stars. The cooking fires were still burning, small heaps of orange and red coals that glowed before the thrusting shadows of the tepees. The smell of roasted meat lingered in the cooling air. The earth was warm under his head, warm and comforting.

He slept in happiness. His life was complete.

He felt the silvered arms of Mother Moon.

Once, in his dreams, he reached out for Little Cousin, and Little Cousin was there.

Curtis

Fort Wade on the Canadian was a nest of soft yellow lights that gleamed warmly against the dark surface of the earth. The night air held the indistinct sounds of music and laughter. Ladders of light spilled out across the parade ground from the open moth-shadowed windows. The lilting music of the orchestra—made up of enthusiastic volunteers from the regimental band—danced through the warm summer air. From the barracks came the clean chords of a strummed guitar.

Fort Wade was celebrating a birthday.

William Foster Curtis was forty-eight years old today.

From the outside, to the men on guard duty, the celebration probably seemed even better than it was. There was something hauntingly nostalgic about a party in the warm summer night, especially if you were on the outside looking in. Yes, and particularly if you were a lonely man. It filled such a man with memories that were not really memories at all but a strange whispered amalgam of events dimly remembered and hopes that had never come true and dreams undead but long denied.

Even Curtis, moving through the center of the party that was in his honor, felt a kind of sadness. He accepted a drink and downed it fast. "Curtis," he said to himself, "it isn't only that you're getting old. You're getting maudlin, and that's one hell of a lot worse."

The party rolled on. The lilt of the music blended cheerfully with the clinking of glasses.

Curtis had a few more drinks and proceeded to lose himself in the noise and the swirl and the fun. He fancied that he was dancing quite well; he was pleased with what he was beginning to regard as a very good sense of rhythm indeed. Why, his leg wasn't bothering him at all—

Quite suddenly, the music stopped.

In the suprised silence, Sergeant Carruthers marched in front of the orchestra. He turned and faced the erstwhile dancers and cleared his throat enormously. "Ladies and gentlemen," he bawled in a parade ground voice, "we have a special treat for you!"

Everyone applauded, including—belatedly—Curtis.

Carruthers cleared his throat again as though afflicted with some tremendous obstruction. He mopped his sweating face. "I have the great honor to present the wife of our colonel," he said. "Ladies and gentlemen, I'm sure you all know Mrs. Helen Curtis." He paused. "Here she is," he concluded lamely and got out of the way.

There were cheers now, cheers and good-natured laughter.

Curtis suddenly realized that most everyone was in on the surprise except himself. To his astonishment, he saw Helen walking gamely up in front of the orchestra, her long blue dress swishing on the floor. And, dear God, she had a guitar tucked under her bare arm. The men in the orchestra were grinning hugely—grinning at him. Helen looked pale, pale and fragile and very pretty.

Curtis glued a smile on his face.

"Friends." Helen said, and stopped. Her voice was constricted with nervousness. She giggled a little. Curtis started to sweat. Helen tried again. "Most of you know that I have been trying to learn to play the guitar."

Everybody laughed, but there was no cruelty in the laughter.

"I wanted to learn a song for a birthday present for my husband," Helen said. "I hope I can play it all the way through."

Curtis manfully widened his smile. He felt as though

he were baring his teeth in a grimace of pain. He hoped to God he didn't look that way.

Helen took a deep breath. "Here goes," she said.

Matt Irvine led a scattering of applause. He radiated confidence. He had heard her play before, of course; his wife had taught her. Curtis noticed that Mary Irvine had her fingers crossed.

Curtis was suddenly very proud of Helen, and ashamed of himself for his embarrassment. She looked so utterly defenseless standing up there in her new blue dress, like a little girl at her first recital. She must have worked very hard, trying to please him. He wanted to go to her, say something to her. But he could not move. She was on her own.

Helen lifted her guitar and struck an introductory chord. It sounded pretty good. Curtis became aware of faces at the windows; some of the men from the barracks had come over to listen. Well, Helen's voice had always been clear and true—

She sang.

"From this valley they say you are going,
"We will miss your bright eyes and sweet smile,
"For they say you are taking the sunshine
"Which has brightened our pathway a while. . . ."

She wasn't bad at all. He had been afraid that she would be awful, and perhaps that made her sound better than she really was. No matter; the quality of her performance wasn't the important thing. Curtis remembered the song. It reached out to him from the past they had shared a very long time ago.

"Come and sit by my side if you love me;
"Do not hasten to bid me adieu.
"But remember the Bright Mohawk Valley,
"And the girl that has loved you so true. . . ."

God, he had not heard those words in many years. In Texas, the song was sung about another place, another river. Sure, the song was trite, had always been trite. That had not mattered then and it did not matter now. He knew that Helen was calling out to him, reaching out along the twisted and separate strands of the years they had spent together. The song was a gift, and more than that. It was an offering.

Helen finished her song. She stood there, awkwardly holding the guitar, smiling at him. The applause was solid and heartfelt.

Curtis started toward his wife. He wanted to thank her somehow, say some of the words that had been too long unspoken—

He didn't make it.

At that moment, at exactly the wrong time, the mess sergeant banged noisily through the door with a cake that was ablaze with candles. He deposited it proudly on a small table. Curtis was shoved forward until he almost fell into the damned thing. Its myriad of candles heated his face. He tried to back away.

The band cut loose with *Happy Birthday*.

Helen made her way to his side, which was all wrong. He wanted to go to her. She touched his arm. Her face was flushed, her eyes bright. "Make a wish, William!" she said. "Make a wish!"

"Blow out the candles!" Matt hollered. "Get 'em all!"

Curtis sucked in some air. He blew a creditable gust at what seemed to be millions of candles. He got most of them on the first try, but not all. He blew again and got the rest. The extinguished candles sent up little blue curls of smoke.

There was a lot of cheering, a lot of noise.

Curtis stared at the smoke that snaked upwards from the blackened candle wicks. He tried to stop thinking, stop remembering. He should have made a wish. There must have been some wish. . . .

"Cut the cake, dear," Helen said.

Curtis reached out and pulled some of the smoking candles from the cake. He crushed them in his hand and dropped the greasy mass to the floor. He sliced the first piece, put it on a plate, and gave it to Helen.

"It's been such a fine party," she whispered.

"It's been a happy birthday," he said. "I won't forget it."

Helen had tears of happiness in her eyes.

Fox Claw

September had come to the Staked Plains. There was no sudden, dramatic change. September slipped in quietly, with a kind of fugitive silence. During the day, the heat of the sun was not as intense as it had been. At night, the air was a little cooler.

That was all.

But the buffalo knew. They were restless now, tasting the wind. When they moved, they moved toward the south.

And Fox Claw knew. His summer was ending. The signs were small, but they were there. Soon the winds would blow from the north and the earth would change. The stars would be frost in the sky and Mother Moon would turn to ice.

He knew that for him there would never be another summer.

He sat with Dies Young in the flickering shadows cast by a small fire. He stared into the flames. "Life is good here," he said.

Dies Young grunted, a black spider in the firelight. Such a remark, he obviously felt, hardly deserved an answer.

Fox Claw did not look at him. "If I go, will you come with me?"

"Why do you go?"

Fox Claw groped for words. "Broken Bow is a good man, but he is old. He has no plan except to go on as long as he can. When the soldiers come, his band will be caught like rabbits in a snare."

"Do you have a plan?"

"I do not want to die like a rabbit."

Dies Young made no reply.

"It has been many seasons since we have been to the canyon of the hard wood. I would go there once more."

"Will things be different there?"

Fox Claw shrugged. "There will be many warriors in the canyon."

Dies Young stood up and stretched. "I am ready when you are ready. Now, I will sleep."

"I will speak with Broken Bow. One day soon, we will ride."

Dies Young moved away and Fox Claw was alone.

For a long time he sat and looked into the fading flames. When the fire was only a bed of orange coals under the stars, he lay down on the ground and closed his eyes.

He was still awake when Little Cousin padded over to him. The dog curled up against his back, gave a puppy sigh of contentment, and dropped off to sleep.

Fox Claw smiled to himself.

There would be three of them going to the canyon.

Palo Duro

South of the sandy flats of the Canadian stretched the plains of northern Texas. It was big country, open country, and it seemed to hold few secrets as it rolled away under the pale blue vault of the sky.

It was a hard land, but it was not truly barren. There were buffalo grasses and grama grasses, and pale green yuccas that thrust stalks of white blossoms into the air. Clumps of lace-leafed mesquite and barbed cat's-claw elbowed the grasses for growing room. After the spring rains, the country was alive with wild flowers: buttercups and Tahoka daisies and flaming paintbrush.

The plains were never empty, never entirely silent. It

was a living land. There was always the stir of the wind. Coveys of quail marched in forked lines, larks sang all day long, and doves called from the cottonwoods that followed the canyon streams. For mile after mile, colonies of prairie dogs had holed the earth. It was too flat and treeless to be good deer country, but it was a rare day when antelope could not be seen, and there were plenty of buffalo. Lobo wolves and coyotes prowled through the grasses, seeking out the cottontails and the mule-eared jack rabbits.

Above it all was the big sky and the great white fireball of the sun.

The plains only seemed to be without mystery. They held their secret, and they had protected it well. This was the land of Palo Duro, the canyon of the hard wood.

The Indians had always known Palo Duro: Comanches and Kiowas and corn-growers and tribes whose very names had been forgotten. Coronado had camped on that canyon floor. Spanish missionaries had gone there to work in the villages. The canyon held the graves of other explorers, marked with the date of 1809. Captain R. B. Marcy had mapped Palo Duro Creek in 1849. For decades, the Comancheros had used the canyon as a center for their outlaw trade with the Indians.

And yet Palo Duro remained a hidden place, a lost world of its own. Only a handful of white men had ever seen it.

Palo Duro was concealed by its very unexpectedness. The flat plains seemed to stretch on endlessly; it was against common sense that a great invisible gash could cut through that hard sun-baked earth. If a man knew about Palo Duro he might be able to sense that shadowed break in the land when he was still several miles away. If he did not know, he could almost ride over the edge of the canyon before he saw it.

The canyon, sliced down through the rock by millions of years of cutting stream water, sculptured into twisted shapes by storms and sand-edged winds, was twenty miles across at its widest point. The floor of the canyon was twelve hundred feet below the canyon rim in some places. The canyon was more than one hundred miles long.

It was not a sheer drop down into Palo Duro. The

canyon walls went down in massive steps, and the slope was usually not too steep to be climbed—if a man were in no great hurry. The walls of the canyon were banded with different kinds and colors of rock. The cap rock was a yellowed caliche. Stripes of gray-white stone ran below the cap rock. Then came bands of ancient shales and sandstones: purple, red, gray, gold, pink, blue, and white. The bottom layers of the walls were a vivid rusty red, and the red clays were shot through with streaks of white gypsum and rock salt. It was the lower part of the canyon walls that gave Palo Duro its dominant color; the canyon had a red glow to it, as though age-old fires burned forever deep within the earth.

The stream that had made Palo Duro was still there—a small creek now, washing slowly over the red clays of the canyon floor. There was other water in Palo Duro, better water that flowed from deep springs. Where there was water, there were trees. Stately cottonwoods grew there, and chinaberry trees, and mesquite with its good beans. There was lots of scrub cedar. The Indians prized the hard cedar wood for their bows and arrows.

Palo Duro was the home of many fantastic things. There were weathered pedestal rocks that looked like stone toadstools. There were colored logs of petrified wood. There were giant bones from great lizards that once had lived on the canyon floor. There were the shells of turtles four feet across. There were cat skulls with teeth like lances. . . .

There were some places where the canyon was fairly narrow and the walls were steep. It was an ideal camping place. Indians of many tribes came to Palo Duro. Sometimes they stayed there for weeks, secure in the knowledge that they were hidden and comfortable and safe from surprise attack.

There was a deceptive feeling of timelessness in Palo Duro. It seemed to be a place in another world, a world in which time as man measured time had no meaning. In all the years the Indians had known Palo Duro it had not visibly changed.

And yet, year by year and inch by inch, the little stream cut more deeply into the red clays of the canyon floor. Even when the spring rains turned the creek into a swollen river of mud it was a slow process—grain by grain, pebble by pebble.

It was very slow.

It took a long time.

But even Palo Duro changed.

Fox Claw

It was late in September when Fox Claw rode into the canyon. At first, Palo Duro looked the same as always.

The white cones of the tepees—Kiowa, Cheyenne, and Comanche—rose in the shade of the tall cottonwoods. There was a good tang of mesquite smoke in the air. The drying racks in the sun were draped with dark meat. The women were busy around the iron cooking pots that bubbled over the fires. Children rushed about gathering firewood and shouting happily. There were plenty of horses and mules grazing in the good grass.

The Kiowas were led by Sky Walker and Lone Wolf, both reliable men. The Cheyennes were under Iron Shirt. The Comanches were from the band of Ohamatai, an old and trusted friend.

Here, if anywhere, Fox Claw thought, there was a chance to take action. There were many warriors.

By the afternoon of the next day, he knew that he had made a mistake. The canyon, perhaps, was as it had always been. But the Indians had changed. They had no stomach for more fighting.

"They have all crawled into a hole," Fox Claw said angrily. "They have not even done it like rabbits who go into the earth to die. They have come here to sleep, to live in a world of dreams. I am tired of dreams."

Dies Young looked at him with affection. His ugly face creased into a smile. "You have not changed, my friend.

As for myself—I will stay here and dream my dreams, or I will ride with you and fight. It is all the same."

Fox Claw sat down on a rock. Even Dies Young did not understand. He could not communicate the thing that burned inside him, the thing that had no name. But Dies Young would follow him, when it came to that. He was not completely alone.

He reached down and scratched at Little Cousin's ears. He looked up at the soaring walls of Palo Duro. Truly, the canyon was an enchanted place, had always been an enchanted place.

It would be good to stay here for a while, to rest and to make what few decisions were left to him.

He said nothing more.

He would make his plans, and then he would do what he had to do.

Curtis

In the early morning hours of the 27th of September, three months to the day after the attack on Adobe Walls, the army came at last to Palo Duro.

In a way, Curtis thought, it was inevitable that the army eventually would clean out the canyon. He had heard stories about Palo Duro, although he had never actually seen it before. He had known that one day he would have to fight there.

Still, it had been a tangled chain of events that had brought the army to Palo Duro at this particular time, on this particular day. Adobe Walls had been the turning point. After the Indian attack on the Walls, the wheels in Washington had finally started to grind. Sheridan got the authority he needed, the authority to crush the Indians by force. The reservations were strictly policed for the first time. The crazy policy of chasing small bands of Indians back and forth across the plains was junked. Sheridan was determined to hit the Indians where they lived, and to hit them with overwhelming firepower. His field commanders—Mackenzie and Miles and Davidson and Curtis—were ordered to converge on the Staked Plains and sweep it clean once and for all.

Palo Duro was the first big step.

The army meant business this time, and it was loaded for bear. Curtis had detached his A and C companies for the attack, but the main striking force was commanded by the ranking colonel, Ranald Mackenzie. Mackenzie had his entire Fourth Cavalry regiment poised to strike, and he had brought along four companies of the Tenth Infantry for good measure.

As Curtis saw it, there was only one serious flaw in Mackenzie as an officer. He was impetuous. His courage made him reckless. Like George Custer, he would charge anything, anywhere, and to hell with the consequences. He had a good record and the Indians feared him, but Mackenzie lost more of his own men than Curtis ever did.

When the striking force came to Palo Duro that September morning, the enemy was in plain sight. The tepees looked like scattered toys on the canyon floor. It was too much for Mackenzie. He wanted to jump down there after them.

Mackenzie jerked his head so hard his hat almost fell off. "Come on, let's get moving. We're wasting time."

The soldiers rode quietly along the stupendous canyon wall, searching for a safe way down. It was bright sunshine up on the plains where they rode, but Palo Duro was still shadowed and gloomy. If any Indian chanced to look up, he would see the blue column outlined sharply against the light sky. Curtis didn't like it. It wasn't his kind of an operation. But he did not question Mackenzie's lead. Mackenzie was in command.

The scouts found a trail. It was an old buffalo path that zigzagged down the wall of the canyon about a mile above the Indian camp. It was a poor trail for a cavalry outfit, but that didn't bother Mackenzie.

"Mr. Thompson," Mackenzie said to his lieutenant in charge of scouts, "take your men down there and open the fight. We will follow by companies, and we'll be breathing down your collar all the way. No matter what happens, you are to keep going down."

Thompson saluted as calmly as though he had just been told to stable the horses back at Fort Concho. Curtis reflected that any man who soldiered for Ranald Mackenzie must have gotten used to hair-raising assignments by now.

Without a word, Lieutenant Thompson took his men and started the long descent into Palo Duro.

One by one, moving in single file, the scouts followed Thompson down. They picked their way slowly along the rock-strewn path, leading their nervous horses. The sun climbed higher into a yellow sky. The walls of the great canyon began to turn red.

Long before the scouts reached the bottom, Mackenzie started the other men down. The whole thing had a strange dreamlike quality to it. There was complete silence except for the clicking of hooves on the rocks and the faint jingle of equipment. The immense canyon was so vast that it seemed unreal. Far away on the canyon floor, the Indian village slept without sound.

Just as Curtis went over the rim at the head of A Company, the good luck of the army was broken. A horse led by one of the scouts kicked against a small boulder and the stone rolled over the cliff. It bounced down the canyon wall and hit with a report that sounded like a cannon shot. The thudding boulder dislodged other rocks, and the whole pile crashed into the floor of Palo Duro and fountained a telltale cloud of reddish dust.

There was at least one Indian who was not asleep. Probably, Curtis thought, he had gotten up early and gone out to look at the horses that were grazing between the village and the trail the soldiers were using. Whoever he was, he let out one wild whoop of alarm and ran down the canyon toward the tepees.

The Indian didn't make it. Lieutenant Thompson's men drilled him neatly before he had run thirty yards.

"That does it," Curtis said to himself.

There was no chance for a surprise now. The Indians reacted with surprising quickness to the sound of the shots, but at first they did not realize what was going on. Warriors stepped out of tepees and stared around blankly, trying to find the source of the shots. By the time they spotted the winding blue column of soldiers and understood the size of the force pitted against them it was too late to cut them off. They were over a mile away at best, and some of them were more distant than that. To make matters worse for the Indians, most of them did not have their horses where they could get to them.

It was a careless camp, Curtis thought. Mackenzie had been lucky.

Curtis continued to pick his way down the trail. The column neither speeded up nor slowed down; it simply kept to its steady pace. Curtis was still high enough on the canyon wall to see the developing action. He watched as the warriors grabbed their weapons and ran toward the soldiers. Their only hope was to delay the advance of the army long enough for their camp to be abandoned. It was a sacrifice, pure and simple. The Indians had been asleep, but they did not hesitate once they had grasped the situation.

Long before there could be any effective resistance, Thompson had his scouts deployed on the floor of Palo Duro to cover the descent of the rest of the army. He stationed his men behind trees and rocks and opened up on the Indian horse herd. The horses went mad with fear and began to race desperately back and forth between the red canyon walls. They kicked up a good cover of protective dust, and the Indians were unable to catch their mounts under the muzzles of Thompson's guns.

The warriors got close enough to shoot but their fire was wild. Their bullets whined through the air and kicked up puffs of dust from the rocks around the blue column moving into the canyon, but they did not hit a man. The rattle of gunfire echoed from the towering canyon walls. Acrid blue-gray powder smoke mixed with the dust and drifted up toward the far sky.

The troops handled themselves well. Curtis was proud of them, proud and excited. It was discipline that made the difference. Raw courage was fine, but it hadn't a chance against precision and training. Curtis felt himself being caught up in the thrill of the attack, and at the same time a part of him watched with detachment, admiring the efficiency of the soldiers.

The army got their horses down into the canyon without a single loss. The men mounted calmly and formed attack lines. They waited. When Mackenzie had three full companies of cavalry in position, he nodded to his bugler. The charge was sounded.

One hundred and eighty men let out a holler and rode hell for leather down the canyon. The exposed front line of the Indians melted like snow in hot water.

Company by company, the remaining troops made their careful way down the old buffalo trail. They assembled in good order, checking their guns. When they charged, they charged in company strength. The dust got so thick that it was almost impossible to see.

The Indians were no strangers to the white man's army. They were afraid for their old people and for their women and children. They fought grimly, doggedly. They did not panic. They climbed the canyon walls like feathered goats and holed up in little pockets of cover behind the rocks, dividing their forces. They pumped bullets and arrows into the dust clouds around the soldiers in a steady stream.

Mackenzie's bugler was hit and pitched from his saddle. Another man fell. A third.

The fire from the rocks got hotter.

The rush of the cavalry was stopped. The men had no massed target to hit, and the withering fire could not be ignored.

Mackenzie was furious. He swore constantly, like a mule-skinner. He wanted to ride straight over that waiting strung-out Indian camp and kill everything in sight. But he couldn't do it. There was nothing for it but to clean out the nests of resisting warriors one by one. It was a dirty business, and it took precious time.

It had to be done.

"Go and get them," Mackenzie ordered Curtis. "Make it fast."

Curtis took over and directed the extermination of the Indian rear guard. He did it his way, not giving a damn what Mackenzie thought about it. He waited until he had his men exactly where he wanted them. He placed troopers high on the canyon wall, above the holed-up Indians. He got them hemmed in from below. Then he opened up on each cluster of warriors, taking them group by group, hitting them with all the massed firepower he could command. It took him an hour and a half. When he was finished, there was no more resistance. He had not lost a man.

Mackenzie was ready to go. He sent his regrouped regiment into a headlong charge down the canyon. He swept through the Indian camp like a scythe, but the village was deserted before he got there. The crumpled tepees were empty and covered with dust. Smashed drying racks lay broken in the sunlight. Iron cooking pots were overturned and left behind. Buffalo robes and discarded clothing were strewn all over the grass. Lodge poles were scattered in the red clay bed of the shallow muddy stream.

A disgusted Mackenzie led his men on down the canyon, but he found no Indians. The old men and the squaws and the children had scaled the canyon walls or had run out through narrow passes to safety. Their trails were plain enough, but there was no way for the cavalry to follow them.

High above them, the red sun was drifting down toward the west. There were already long black shadows striping the floor of Palo Duro. The air was clogged with gritty red dust. Mackenzie had wounded men to consider. It would have been folly to try to press home a night attack, and Mackenzie was not stupid. The Indians knew where they were now. Not all of their fighting men had been killed in the canyon. They had had plenty of time to set up an ambush in terrain that was suicide for the cavalry. They would be waiting, in a place of their own choosing.

Enough was enough.

But Mackenzie wasn't through yet. He gave quick orders to round up the Indian horses and get them out of the canyon before dark. Then he turned to Curtis. "I have one more job for you. I will see to the wounded myself. I want you to keep your men down here in the canyon until we get out with the horses. We'll take your mounts along with us. When the canyon is clear, fire the tepees and then climb out and join us on the rim. I don't want a single tepee left standing when you leave here. Understood?"

Curtis felt a sudden coldness in his stomach. His hands began to sweat slightly. He didn't want this job. But his pale eyes remained steady.

"Understood," he said.

Curtis walked off to give his orders to Matt and Captain Taylor. Then he sat down on a rock to wait. He did not smoke his pipe.

The men of A and C Companies made two large fires and then rested. It was quite dark before Mackenzie got all of the horses and mules up the steep trail and over the cap rock. The great walls of the canyon lost their color. The far velvet sky frosted over with stars. Palo Duro was as still as death except for the yelping of coyotes on the black cliffs.

Curtis got to his feet and took a deep breath.

"All right, gentlemen," he said quietly. "Let's build our fire."

He felt a terrible coldness as he watched his men take burning sticks from the fires they had prepared. He shivered as though he were in the middle of a norther. He did not want to watch, but he could not take his eyes away. The men moved like shadowy ghosts from tepee to tepee. They threw dead wood and dry brush into the Indian lodges. They laughed and shouted as they put the torch to them.

At first, the flames caught slowly, reluctantly. But the fires were set well; they did not go out. As soon as the lodge poles ignited, the tepees burned with an increasing roar. A stink of scorched hides filled the night air.

In less than an hour, the great village was an inferno. The crackling tepees burned like strange conical torches. The grass began to burn, and the trees. A stir of wind blew through the canyon and fanned the flames. Tepees began to collapse with showers of orange sparks. The old wood of the lodge poles cracked with loud reports as the licking flames found their hearts.

It was hot in the canyon, hot with the dry searing heat of fire. Greasy smoke hung in Palo Duro like strange clouds, sealing off the distant sky. A camp three miles long can make a lot of smoke when it burns.

Curtis shut his eyes against the heat. He clenched his fists.

He could still see it. He could not escape from it by closing his eyes. He saw it, smelled it, felt it.

It all came back.

He remembered.

He remembered all of it. He had never forgotten. He had shut it away from him, locked it into a compartment in his brain, but it had always been with him.

It had been during the War, of course. So many things had happened during the War; the War had changed everything. He had been tired, very tired, and he had seen too many of his men shot to pieces. Excuses? No, there were no excuses. There could be no excuses. He had done what he had done.

He remembered.

The southern night had been warm and heavy with the smell of flowers. There had been a moon, a full moon. And a great white-pillared house that had stood on a hill that was carpeted with soft smooth grass.

The house had been searched, but something drew him to it. He had gone in alone. He hadn't known why; it may have been nothing more than a desire to go into a real house again. He remembered how big it had seemed, how different from the dirty tents he had known for so long. He could smell the books and the curtains and the polish on the chairs.

It had been dark in the house, but he had found them. They were hiding behind racks of clothes in a big closet in one of the bedrooms. A boy had come at him with a pistol. He had been too young and terrified to do what he tried to do. Curtis killed him with his saber.

That left the woman and the baby.

The woman said something to him. He didn't remember what it had been, even now.

Curtis went mad. He snapped, completely. He ripped the baby out of the woman's arms and threw the baby back into the closet. He raped the woman on the floor, like an animal. When he came to his senses, the woman was dead. He had choked her to death.

He set fire to the house, hardly knowing what he was doing. The house was dry and dusty and burned very fast. He ran away, crying.

He was sick, sick in the soft grass with the moon shining down on him. He shook like an old man with fever. He remembered, just as his men came running up to see about the burning house. There had been a baby—

He ran back into the house, shouting insanely. He was scorched by the flames. He choked on the smoke. He went back into that room. He wrapped the baby in his coat and ran out again before the roof fell in.

He had been a hero. Everyone said so.

The baby had died the next morning.

The fires of Palo Duro brought it all back. He could never escape from it.

Curtis opened his eyes and looked directly at the crackling flames. He shuddered. He thought of Helen, and what she thought he was. He thought of other things.

He was not the only man who had done such a thing in the War. He was not the first man who had discovered that a dark stranger lived inside his own body, waiting to take over.

If he could face it, really face it—

Matt's voice. Steady, uncomprehending. "All ready, Bill. Time we were clearing out of here."

Curtis pulled himself back. He nodded. "Very good, Matt. Let's go."

They climbed out of the burning canyon on foot. It was a long hot climb. Curtis could feel the heat from the flames on his back. The smoke from the canyon made him cough and brought tears to his eyes. When they reached the canyon rim, all of the men turned and looked back.

The floor of Palo Duro was alive with orange rivers of flame. The firelight gleamed through the dirty smoke and was reflected from the red walls of the canyon. The place was hell's own oven. The heat was so intense it could be felt on the cap rock.

It was not the same canyon that Curtis had seen that morning. Palo Duro was a scar in the earth.

The fires burned all night.

Fox Claw

Dies Young was asleep. He could sleep anywhere, under any conditions. But Fox Claw was wakeful. He stood on the canyon rim and watched Palo Duro burn.

Fox Claw was about six miles from where the soldiers were camped. He had been there throughout the battle. He had not fired a shot.

He had ridden out of the canyon on the previous night with Little Cousin on his saddle. Dies Young had followed him; to go or to stay was all the same to him. Fox Claw had left for a very simple reason. He could no longer bear to stay in Palo Duro.

There had been no premonition, no hint of coming danger. It was just that he had had enough of false dreams. The Indians camped in the canyon had not been real; they had been enchanted men. They were not interested in raiding. They were not even interested in posting sentries to guard against attack. They moved in a haze of unreality, without acting, without thinking. They existed, and that was enough for them.

Fox Claw had tried to arouse them. He had warned them and he had tried to tell them as best he could of the things that were in his heart. They had not listened. They had not cared.

Fox Claw rode away. What he had sought in Palo Duro he had not found. He did not choose to wait in his hole like a rabbit. He was determined that when the time came for him to trade his life he would get something in return.

All that long day he had watched. Now the night had come, and the canyon was in flames.

He watched it burn.

He stood very still on the canyon rim and stared at

the fire. He smelled the stink that boiled up out of the earth.

He thought: *Once this place was mine. Once it was a part of the land I knew. Now it is gone. When the light comes again, I will not see the green trees and the good grass. I will see ashes and fire-blackened skeletons.*

It is gone, like all the rest. It is stone; it will not remember. One day, it may be green again, and the water good to drink. Even white men cannot burn a whole canyon.

But I will never see it.

For me it is gone.

It was morning when he rode away from Palo Duro. He and Dies Young said no words; there was nothing to say. His hand stroked Little Cousin as he rode.

His dark eyes were cold.

Palo Duro

The white sun climbed slowly through the sky above the smoking gash of Palo Duro, and then it drifted down again toward the western horizon. For the sun, nothing had changed.

Tule Canyon was not far away; to the sun looking down the two canyons were one. The bodies of the dead horses and mules, shot by Mackenzie because he could not hold them, were swelling in the heat. Wolves and coyotes began to circle more closely on padded paws. Black clouds of buzzards slanted down out of the great blue sky.

Palo Duro was vast, and it would endure. In time, the forces that had made Palo Duro a living thing would make it green again. The seasons would pass, and the winds and the rains would erase the thing that men had done there.

The floor of Palo Duro would cool. It would only take a moment as Palo Duro measured time. The little creek that wound through the canyon would be fresh and clean, someday. The long silences between the red canyon walls would come again.

The bones of the horses in Tule Canyon would dry and be bleached by the sun. They would be there for awhile. Charlie Goodnight would ride right past them in 1876 when he herded two thousand head of Texas Longhorns into Palo Duro to start a cattle ranch. One day, there would be wild roses in Palo Duro. Charlie Goodnight's wife would look after them, visiting them day after day. Then the spring rains would come, as they always came, and there would be a cave-in from the high cliffs. The roses would die. There would be a place in Palo Duro known as *Lagrimas de la Rosa*—Tears of the Rose.

Palo Duro was eternal. It would survive through all the years of time to be, and perhaps it would not forget.

But the years pass slowly, day by day. For now there were only the fine white ashes that settled thickly on the rust-red clays, and the sound of black wings that floated down out of the sky toward the canyon of the hard wood.

Curtis

After the fight at Palo Duro, Curtis returned to Fort Wade but he did not stay there long. Within a week he rode out again, headed for Fort Sill.

He had plenty of good reasons for going to Sill. The power of the Indians in the southern plains had been broken for good, but there was still a lot of mopping-up to do. He needed to consult with Davidson in order to coordinate their operations. He wanted to see for himself the changes that had taken place on the reservation.

There was no shortage of reasons. A man could always think up reasons.

Of course, they were not the real reasons.

He rode into Fort Sill with a slight smile on his face.

He was thinking of all the biographies he had read of famous men—yes, and of the autobiographies too. The motives of such men were always so neat and clear and simple. Always logical. Always involved with the big events of their time.

"In early October, 1874, Colonel Curtis rode from Fort Wade to Fort Sill in order to consult with Colonel Davidson of the Tenth Cavalry. The remaining Indians on the Staked Plains posed a knotty problem in tactics, and. . . ."

And Maria?

Well, the Marias of the world seldom found their way into biographies, much less autobiographies.

But they were there, in the shadows. They pulled the strings.

Curtis would go talk to Davidson again. That, perhaps, was for his biographer, if he ever had one.

Then he would go to Maria.

That was for him.

It was a cold night, cold and frosted with stars. The silence was frozen, waiting for the northers of winter. Curtis had on his heavy overcoat when he slipped out of Sill, but he had to walk fast just to keep warm.

He did not think about the fact that this was the last time he would ever take this walk. Possibly, he didn't believe it. He thought of Maria and the warm house and the silk of her hair. It was just as it had always been.

And yet, it was different. He knew it before he reached her house. The night was not the same. He was not the same, not quite.

He quickened his pace when he saw her house. He was almost running.

The gray boards of the unpainted shack were ghostly in the starlight. The house looked small somehow, smaller than he had remembered, small and lost in the hush of the night. It looked cold and lonely. He had never seen it that way before, that house of warmth and life. He suddenly thought that he might be seeing it for the first time through Maria's eyes. It was just a poor shack, and the life it sheltered had not been a happy one—

There were no lights showing.

He knocked on the door. The thin boards gave slightly under his fist. The sound of his knocking was empty and hollow.

"Maria!" he called.

There was no answer.

He pounded on the door until it shook on its hinges. There was no sound from inside, no welcoming splash of yellow light from the lamp, no rich liquid voice calling out to him.

Then he saw it.

There was a heavy padlock on the outside of the wooden door.

Curtis felt a stab of bitter cold run through him. Quickly, he walked around the little shack. All of the windows were boarded up.

The house was empty.

Where had she gone? Curtis thought he knew. She had people in San Antonio. She had often talked of going back there, back to the hot sun and the markets and the river. There was a man there, a good man who had wanted to marry her and give her children. Curtis had seen him once—a tall Mexican with proud eyes and a high-crowned hat faded from the sun. Perhaps she had gone to him. Or perhaps she had gone to one of the big houses in San Antonio. They always needed women. A good whore could make a lot of money for a few years, and the life wasn't too rough. And then, when she got older. . . .

He turned and started back toward Sill.

It was a long, cold walk. He did not look back.

The next afternoon was a memorable one at Fort Sill.

Curtis did not often feel that he was a part of history, or a witness to historical events. Things happened too fast for that, and they were swallowed up in masses of detail that obscured their significance. It was a rare thing for him to be able to stand back and watch something with a sense of perspective.

This time he knew, and he watched with fascination.

He stood in the warm sun with Davidson and Samuel Reed and stared at the unfinished icehouse. It had a solid stone floor and high stone walls but no roof. The ice house was full of Indians, and it stank to high heaven.

They were waiting for the escort column and for Kicking Bird.

Kicking Bird came first, riding up on the handsome gray horse that had been given to him by his officer friends at Sill. Curtis had to hand it to him. If he had been Kicking Bird he wouldn't have had the guts to show up at all.

The Kiowa nodded a greeting and dismounted. He stood quietly by his horse. He seemed sad rather than nervous. Everyone knew what Kicking Bird had done. He was a famous man.

After Adobe Walls, things had changed at Fort Sill. When the Indian survivors had drifted back to the reservation, there had been no sympathy for them, and no forgiveness. The Indians were herded like wild animals into the old stone corral at Sill. Everything was taken from them: their horses, their weapons, their saddles, their food, their pride. The soldiers had shot seven hundred and fifty of their horses before the resulting smell had caused a policy change; the rest had been sold at auction for a fraction of their value. Everything else was piled in heaps and burned.

Some of the Indians, like Ishatai, had gotten back before the army took over the reservation. Most of them had not been that lucky. Over one hundred warriors had been placed in the icehouse. Once a day, the quartermaster dispatched a wagon to the icehouse and the soldiers threw chunks of raw meat over the walls to keep the prisoners alive.

The new orders were clear and concise. All friendly Indians—that is to say, all those who were afraid or unwilling to fight—had to be enrolled by name and answer to regular inspections. Indians thought to be guilty of raiding were tried and punished—and a man was guilty if he could not prove his innocence.

When the army had run into trouble in finding small parties of Indians that were still off the reservation, Kicking Bird had volunteered his services. He organized his own scouting groups. He was very effective. He talked his people into coming in, explaining to them at some length about brotherhood and the futility of continued resistance. He appeared to be genuinely sorry when many of them were locked up in the icehouse.

The long chain of command had worked hard, helping Kicking Bird in his efforts to solve the Indian problem. A plan was developed by Phil Sheridan, passed on to Sherman, and approved by President Grant. The worst Indians were to serve as object lessons for the rest. They were to be shipped out to the coast of Florida and imprisoned in old Fort Marion in Saint Augustine.

There was only one small problem. Who *were* the worst Indians?

The invaluable Kicking Bird volunteered his services again. It caused him much sorrow, but he agreed to select the Indians to be sent to Saint Augustine. He picked out seventy-four Kiowas, Comanches, and Cheyennes. He said that his heart was troubled, but it seemed clear to him that someone had to send the bad Indians away if the good Indians like Kicking Bird were to have a chance to walk the white man's road.

And now he waited in the warm afternoon sun, standing quietly by the fine gray horse the white men had given to him.

Curtis heard the creaking of the approaching wagons. He pulled out his pipe and lit it. He approved of the new policy; he had suggested much the same thing himself many times. But it was a sad thing to watch, and he found it impossible to admire what Kicking Bird had done.

The column of wagons drew up in front of the icehouse and halted. The men of the escort detail unlocked the icehouse door. They ordered the Indians out.

The prisoners were a sorry looking lot. They were chained hand and foot. They were filthy and skinny and their clothes were rags. They could not bring themselves to look at the land they were leaving. They stared down at their feet.

Kicking Bird mounted his gray horse and held up his right hand. He spoke to the miserable group of Indians. He called them his brothers. He told them how sorry he was that this thing had to happen. He explained that they had brought it all on themselves. He promised them that he would work for their early release.

Curtis breathed the stink from the icehouse and tried to keep from throwing up.

Kicking Bird's speech was greeted by total silence.

After what seemed a very long time, one of the prisoners lifted his head. He looked at Kicking Bird. He held up his chained hands. "You have done well, Kicking Bird," he said softly. "Enjoy your freedom. It will not be for long."

Kicking Bird waved his hand.

The Indians were loaded into the wagons. The column rolled jerkily away toward Caddo Crossing.

Kicking Bird turned in his saddle and looked at Samuel Reed. "That man," he said in a very low voice, "that Mamanti. He will make medicine against me."

Sam Reed tried to speak with a confident voice. "You have nothing to fear from witch magic," he said. "That is all in the past."

Kicking Bird did not reply. He just rode away on his fine gray horse.

Curtis had a definite feeling that he wouldn't be seeing Kicking Bird again.

There was a terrible stillness in the afternoon air.

"Well, that's that," Davidson said, rubbing his hands together. "Let's get away from this smell."

Yes, Curtis thought. *Yes, let's get away from it—if we can*.

Tomorrow, he would ride back to Fort Wade.

Fox Claw

Suddenly, the soldiers were everywhere.

Fox Claw had known that the soldiers were coming. After Palo Duro, it had only been a matter of time. He was not dismayed at the numbers of soldiers he saw. It made no real difference to him.

But he was surprised.

The thin blue columns crossed and recrossed the old trails of the Staked Plains like ants.

It was hard to believe that the old days were gone forever—hard to believe that something so eternal, so much a part of the texture of life itself, could disappear in a few brief months. But a man could not deny the evidence of his own eyes. Fox Claw's summer under the big sky, that summer that stretched from Adobe Walls to Palo Duro, had been a kind of dream, a dream that sealed the present from the past, a dream in which a man could still live as a man should live. But it had been a short dream after all. There were now more soldiers on the Staked Plains than there were Indians.

After Palo Duro, the Staked Plains had been all that remained of the home of The People. Now even this was threatened.

It was hard just to survive, just to go on living. There were few safe camping places left for the small band of Broken Bow. They had to move very carefully. The soldiers always seemed to be waiting for them; the band would spend days searching out a remembered spring only to find the soldiers camped there before them. The army had converged on the Staked Plains from every direction.

There was no rest. The Indians were constantly harried, constantly on the move. They could not light even a little fire to warm themselves on the cool, damp nights. They were always hungry. They could not hunt. They were the hunted.

The People did not complain. They simply fell into long silences and stared at nothing. The old men died, one by one. The women could no longer laugh. Many of the children were sick with swollen bellies.

It was October on the Staked Plains.

The land was beautiful again, and deceptively peaceful. The earth was dotted with small blue lakes of sweet rainwater from the Canadian to the Pecos. There was a fresh smell to the air. It was a different world from the parched brown hardness of summer. The dry stream beds that the children had played in were filled with living water.

The buffalo—those that were left—began to drift back toward the south, away from the knife-edged winds of the northern winter.

The water made the Staked Plains soft and easy again. The land was too easy. It drew the searching soldiers as a dead buffalo attracted the flies.

Fox Claw was not afraid; he had left all fear behind him long ago. As the land changed with the ancient rhythm of the seasons, Fox Claw changed with it. He was a part of the land, as much a part of it as the rocks and the sand and the grass. He shed his lazy summer skin like a snake. He lost the few extra pounds that the hot summer had left him. The cold winds hardened and sharpened him, as though he were a rock being stripped of its coating of summer dust.

His time for fighting had come again. That was well. Fox Claw was ready to make his fight.

Broken Bow was not so eager. He was an old man and he had the quiet patience of experience. In a way, his years had tricked him. In his heart he believed that nothing had really changed, that nothing could ever change basically. He had led his people with great skill, surprising even Fox Claw with his knowledge of the land he called his home. In the parched summer days, he had always known where to dig for water when there was no sign of moisture in the hard-baked desert sands. Now, with the army all around him, he could move like a shadow past the blue lakes, seeking the hidden water holes. He had the cunning of an animal that had been hunted through many seasons, and he had survived. He was convinced that he could hold out forever. He could hide. Perhaps, one day, the army would go away as mysteriously as it had come. Broken Bow would still be there. For him, that was enough.

It was not enough for Fox Claw. He knew that the white man would never leave. He knew that the land could never be his again. He had lived his last free summer. All that remained was to die. The only choice that had been given to him was in the way he chose to die. He had made that choice.

He could pick his time.

That was all.

The night came quickly.

The Kwahadis made camp by a cold little pond. The starlight glittered on the black water and outlined the warriors clearly against the dark earth, but Broken Bow had chosen his place well. The water had gathered in a small depression that was lower than the level of the surrounding plains. The camp was in a kind of bowl, and the horizons of the night were close and above them on all sides. They could not be seen unless a man rode up to the very rim of the bowl and looked down.

Broken Bow was wise. The camp was safe. The croaking of the frogs was so loud that it covered the sound of their voices.

They ate tough dry pemmican and washed it down with cold water from the prairie pool. They spread out their buffalo robes for warmth and watched the moon float up through a sea of stars. Ai-eee, Mother Moon! She was a mother of ice this night.

Fox Claw had to make an effort of will to shake off a dreamlike feeling of unreality. It would have been easy just to sleep. It would have been easy to forget a little longer. But he moved. Slowly and deliberately, he did what he had to do. He knew there was a kind of madness in his actions. He sensed that he had somehow lived past his time. The world around him was not his world. The natural movements of his life had once been right and inevitable, like the growing of the grass or the unfolding of a flower. Now these same movements had subtly changed; they had taken on a different quality. He had to force himself now, he had to think about what he did. He had to remember each step he made, consider it with care, as in the performance of a childhood dance. His movements had become a kind of ritual, a ritual that he consciously enacted. His actions were a medicine web that he spun between himself and a world he could not wholly understand.

Fox Claw painted himself for war.

He tied a strip of red cloth to his lance and tipped the lance with two eagle feathers.

He saddled Watcher and mounted.

Fox Claw rode out alone to the rim of the basin, not speaking to anyone. He made no pleas, offered no arguments. Out on the rim he lifted his lance. His dark figure was silhouetted against the cold blaze of the stars. It was cold, cold and lonely. But horse and rider were one; there was no need for communication between them. Watcher moved without urging, walking in a slow circle along the ridge that surrounded the camp. Fox Claw sat rigidly in his saddle, holding his lance high above his head.

It was the ancient call to battle.

"Come!" he whispered into the black silence of the night. "Who will ride with Fox Claw?"

He felt a curious splitting sensation as though he had suddenly divided into two people. Fox Claw rode in terrible isolation around the basin rim, feeling the power of Watcher between his legs and the cold kiss of the wet night air against his face. And another Fox Claw stood down in the camp of Broken Bow looking up at that solitary rider who brushed the stars with his feathered lance.

He spoke again, softly: "Come! Who will ride with Fox Claw?"

But no one came. There was no answer to the call of his lance. The camp of Broken Bow was silent.

Fox Claw stopped, framed by the moon. He kept his lance held high. He waited. He was very cold. Time stopped.

His arm ached with the weight of the lance. The stars moved above him.

There was a movement in the camp below. One dark figure detached itself from the rest. The figure moved without sound, as in a dream. It gathered up a bow and a lance. It saddled a horse and mounted. The horse carried the figure up to the ridge on muffled hooves. The horse stopped by Fox Claw's side.

Dies Young had come. The two men spoke no greeting.

They waited together. It did not seem so cold now.

Slowly, very slowly, one more man began to move in the camp of Broken Bow. The man took a long time, making himself ready. He cut out his horse and rode up to the basin rim, stopping beside Fox Claw and Dies Young. Fox Claw recognized River Smoke in the moonlight. He was surprised; he did not know River Smoke well. River Smoke was young, almost as young as Buffalo Tongue. . . .

The three men waited.

The village in the hollow below was a camp of the dead. There was no sound in it and no motion.

No one else came to join them.

Time began again.

Fox Claw lowered his lance. His arm felt heavy and sluggish as the blood poured into it. His face was expressionless. He had not hoped for more; he was beyond hope. But a man can expect the worst, and it still hurts when it comes. Two men! Two men who would ride with Fox Claw. It was more than a knife-thrust at his pride. Once, pride had been almost everything, but that was past. This raid was different. This was a ride into the old ways, a ride into tradition, a ride back into the heart of the way of The People. This was a ritual, a closing of the circle. Not long ago there had been thousands of warriors ready to strike through other nights and other years, ready to ride with their backs straight and their heads held high. Now there were three.

Mother Moon would be lonely this night.

"I am ready," Fox Claw said.

He wheeled Watcher around and rode away from the camp of Broken Bow. He did not look back. He felt a sudden release, a breaking away from a life he had not chosen. He was almost happy.

It came to Fox Claw, in the stillness of the cold night, that there were not many warriors left, not in all the great world of the South Plains. Perhaps there were only three, and he was their leader. That was something. It might be that Mother Moon would understand.

They rode at a steady pace and Fox Claw's heart lightened with every step that Watcher took. Numbers were not everything. He was taking action. He was free. . . .

But they had not gone far before the pale fingers of dawn began to streak the eastern sky ahead of them. That was when it happened, in that magic moment that divides the night from the coming day.

There is a fragile hush that tautens the earth just before the cries of the birds begin. That tense silence was shattered by a sudden spine-shivering howl.

The riders stopped, instantly.

The howl had been very close. It was a deep-throated cry, infinitely mournful. It was repeated four times. There was no mistaking it. It was the call of a wolf.

Fox Claw felt his hackles rise. It was not fear that he felt. It was something deeper than fear. It was the sense of awe that engulfs a man when he stands in the presence of the unearthly.

The wolf had called four times. . . .

"He speaks to us," Dies Young whispered.

"Yes. We will listen."

The predawn hush tightened to the breaking point. Nothing moved in all the world. The three riders were motionless. Even the sun seemed to have stopped, for the sky grew no lighter. Fox Claw felt the icy sweat rise in the palms of his hands.

The hidden wolf howled again. Ah, it was a strangely human cry the wolf had; there was the soul of a man in it. Once it called, then twice, three times—

Four.

That was all. The long silence came again, deeper than before. The silence was the taut hush of the gathering storm. It held in suspension all the sounds and presences of life waiting to be born.

The sun moved. It grew lighter.

Fox Claw took a deep breath, breaking the spell.

"We go back," he said quietly.

There was no argument. Fox Claw had not expected any. He was the war leader, even if the raiding party consisted of only three men. There could be no talking against him.

His mind was in a turmoil. He rode through the golden morning with blind eyes. Were even the spirits against him now?

The wolf was more than an animal. All of The People knew that the wolf was their brother. He was a deeper and more mysterious kinsman than the prankster coyote. There had always been close ties between the wolf and the Comanches. When the wolf called to a war party it meant danger.

And if the wolf called in a series of four, and did it *twice*. . . .

The war party had to turn back. That was all. That had always been the way, and now it was more urgent than ever. This raid had to be done properly. This time, of all times, the call of the wolf could not be ignored. It would be a disaster to go on, but there was more at stake than that. It would be a violation, an arrogance, a flaunting of the way.

Fox Claw could not believe that the spirits were against him. He did not dare to believe it. No, it must be that his brother was watching over him. The wolf knew everything. Fox Claw had taken his name from one who was close to the wolf. The wolf too would know about Little Cousin, waiting back at the camp of Broken Bow. There was a web of kinship here, a network of magical ties that knit together man and beast, earth and sky, sun and stars. The wolf was helping him. Fox Claw was not alone. He was riding an old, old trail, and there are always friends that camp along the old trails that wind back into the past.

He rode away from the sun with the light of morning filling the sky behind him. He was shaken but he was not discouraged. It was not easy to have faith now, not easy to believe. But this was a deeper thing than the words of an Ishatai. The wolf could not lie. A man could not doubt the things that were certain, the things that had always been true.

There was still time for what must be done.

There was still time to be a man.

Mother Moon would rise again.

The next night there was no sign of the wolf. The three warriors rode through the darkness like phantoms. When the sun turned the edges of the eastern clouds to flame, they stopped and holed up for the day. They seemed to melt into the welcoming earth; they had been transformed into nocturnal beings who vanished with the touch of the sun.

All through the following night they rode, making no more sound than the cool wind that whispered through the October night. They slept again, and then they were ready.

Fox Claw led them through a magical world of silver and black while the waning moon raced above them. The night was friendly around him; the night was his. All of his senses were tautened to an almost supernatural pitch. He saw every white stone and every black stand of brush. He heard the rustle and scurry of each small animal he passed. He felt the rush of an owl's wings on his face as the owl glided down low, skimming the earth, searching for mice. He felt his own warm blood flowing through his veins. It was never really dark beneath the stars, not even after the moon was gone. Except for color and distance, he could see better than he could in the harsh light of day.

Fox Claw never paused, never hesitated. His memory was good. He knew where he was going.

He remembered the small square ranch house that stood alone, so far from its neighbors. He remembered how the blue smoke curled up into the sky out of the black pipe in the sod roof. He remembered how the soft yellow light spilled from the glass windows at night. He remembered the five tired horses nodding their heads in the log corral.

Fox Claw remembered the people who lived in that dugout house. He had seen them many times. The man with his dirty sun-faded hat and the great gnarled hands that roped out of the long sleeves of his patched gray shirt. The long-haired boy, all arms and legs, carrying the fresh-cut fragrant firewood to the house. And the woman. He remembered the white woman with her long blue cotton dress. He could see her standing at the kitchen door, her gold hair pulled back in a knot on her head, shielding her eyes with her thin hand, looking for her man. Many times he had watched her. He knew that she was afraid. To her, the night was no friend. To her, the night was a dark sea of shadows, a black well of terror that sealed her in a pit of nameless dread.

Why had she come? Why had any of them come? What made them stay in an alien land?

He grunted. *He* had not asked them to come. They were the killers of the way, the destroyers of the dream. The soldiers had come to protect people like them. If they were gone, if they had never come—

But they were here. They waited at the end of the night. . . .

The warriors reached the small ranch house just at dawn, as Fox Claw had planned. They dismounted and crept toward the house, moving through the tricky light that divides the night from the day. The stars had faded in the pale sky above them.

The ranch dog began to bark querulously. He did not bark long; he had not really caught their scent. The gentle morning breeze was in their faces.

They waited, making no sound.

The red sun lifted slowly over the horizon. The sky turned white and then pale blue. A rooster crowed in the bare-scratched hen yard, and kept on crowing. He made enough noise to wake the dead. His efforts were rewarded by a puff of black smoke that gushed out of the pipe in the sod roof. The black smoke gradually changed to a thin stream of blue that washed away in the breeze.

They waited.

The boy came out first, rumpled and rubbing his eyes. Then the man walked out of the back door with his hat on. He had a pipe clamped between his teeth. He had no gun.

They waited, letting them get well away from the house.

Fox Claw was very calm. He raised himself on his elbow, taking a careful bead just below the man's hat.

"Now," he said.

He fired, the guns of Dies Young and River Smoke crashed with his. The man spun around and his hat fell off. He fell to the ground, hitting hard. He got up and fell again. He started to crawl back toward the house. The boy cried out once, then caught his father around the shoulders and tried to lift him.

Fox Claw nodded.

The three warriors leaped to their feet and raced across the night-damp ground. They screamed wildly, unconsciously, not even knowing that they screamed. They knocked the boy into the dirt and went after the man.

The man's eyes were still open. His great hand fumbled for a rock. Dies Young threw himself on him, smothering him, and his knife flashed in the sun. The man moaned once and that was all.

River Smoke caught the boy and held him. The boy was too terrified to use the strength he had. He sobbed and twisted and tried to bite River Smoke.

Dies Young got up with his knife dripping red.

Fox Claw looked at the boy and said nothing. The time for taking captives was long past. He turned away. He heard it when the boy stopped crying.

There was no sign of the dog now.

With a noise that was louder because of its surprise, a big gun boomed from the doorway of the ranch house. A slug slammed into a shed behind them kicking up sharp white splinters.

Dies Young dropped down behind the body of the man he had knifed. River Smoke ducked back into the shed. Fox Claw smiled a little and fell down on his belly. He wormed his way into the grass that surrounded the house. The rifle boomed again and he heard the bullet cutting the air over his head. The woman could not shoot. Fighting women was easy work.

He crawled through the grass until he reached the side of the house. He scrambled to his feet and went in a crouching run along the side of the house away from the back door where the woman was. He ran through a small garden. He tried the front door. It was open. The woman was not thinking well.

Silent as a shadow, he slipped into the house. The stink of the white man was strong; the odor of heavy soap almost made him sick. He walked on silent feet between chairs and a wooden table. He stepped into the kitchen.

She did not see him. He caught her from behind by the long gold hair that had not yet been tied up on her head. He knocked the rifle out of her hands with one sharp blow.

She screamed like an animal.

She kept on screaming, mindlessly.

The noise bothered him. He wanted it to stop. Still holding her hair tightly with his left hand, he reached out with his right and seized her around the neck. Her neck was very thin. He closed his strong fingers. The screams stopped.

He threw her on the floor. She lay there gasping, her white eyes bulging from their sockets. She had no color. Her body twitched uncontrollably. Her mouth was open but no sound came from it.

He stood quite still, looking down at her.

Dies Young and River Smoke came in through the kitchen door. They stopped. Dies Young was impassive; he might have been looking at a dead buffalo. River Smoke began to breathe harder. He had never been this close to a white woman before.

The two warriors made no move. They waited for Fox Claw to act. He was the leader.

Slowly, Fox Claw knelt down and touched the woman's thin arm. The flesh felt dead. It was as cold as ice. She opened her mouth wider, trying to scream. Her teeth were very small, very white. She smelled of soap. Fox Claw reached out and took her soft gold hair in his hard hand. He tried to smile.

The woman fainted. Her body gave a little jerk under her twisted dress and was still. Her mouth closed with an audible click.

For a moment Fox Claw made no move. Then he stood up and turned away. He did not want her. He was sick. He felt as if he were going to vomit. It was the smell of the soap. It must be the smell of the soap.

Dies Young looked at him and said nothing.

Fox Claw heard River Smoke make a noise deep in his throat. It was an inhuman sound, the growl of a beast. He heard the tearing noise of the woman's cotton dress.

"Give me your knife," he said to Dies Young.

He did not know why he said it. He had a knife of his own. But the knife of Dies Young had already been used twice this day. It could be used again.

Dies Young gave it to him.

Fox Claw turned quickly, dropping to one knee. He

ignored River Smoke. He cut the woman's throat with one quick slice. He stood up and returned the knife to Dies Young.

"It is done," he said. "Let us get the horses."

The two warriors walked out of the house. River Smoke, holding himself away from the blood, watched them go with shocked disbelief.

River Smoke stayed where he was for a long time. Then, slowly, he left the dead woman on the floor and followed them outside.

Fox Claw did not speak to him. He had nothing to say. He did not understand why he had done what he had done. There had been no reason for him to deny River Smoke the white woman.

He had done it. That was all.

Inside the ranch house, the tall coffeepot was still bubbling cheerfully on top of the wood stove.

Curtis

Hunter and hunted.

It was the oldest game in the history of the world. If it went on long enough, it always had the same ending.

The gray of October faded into November and the wind had cold teeth in it as it whined across the naked brown flatlands of the Staked Plains. The close sky was heavy with clouds the color of lead and the fires of the sun were thin.

Curtis rode at the head of a weary A Company, his heavy coat adding to the ache in his shoulders. The coat did not warm him; he was always cold. His leg was exposed to the chilling winds and it pained him, but he said nothing. His face turned to leather in the wind; it became a frozen mask that felt nothing at all. It seemed to him that he had been riding forever. The land had blurred before his eyes until it was all the same, without feature or interest or change. He was bone tired.

There was only one difference now.

The hunter knew his prey.

Curtis had learned the name of Fox Claw.

The murder of the Dawson family had stunned the frontier. It was an archetype, the stuff that legends were made of. It could not be forgotten.

Such stories, it seemed to Curtis, always had a logic, a kind of mystique, of their own. They were always complete. They were always known down to the last tiny detail. Some of the details were probably wrong, of course, but most of them had the ring of truth about them. He could not imagine how such things became known. But, sometimes, they did.

It was known that a Comanche named Fox Claw had led the raid. It was known that a man named Dies Young had been with him, riding with Fox Claw like a shadow. It was known that a third man had been along, a young man, but his name had been lost.

Perhaps someone had seen them, riding under the moon. Someone, somewhere, must have recognized them before or after the attack on the Dawson ranch house. No one knew for sure. No one bothered to track it down. It didn't matter.

The name was known. Fox Claw.

Curtis knew more than the name of the man he hunted. He knew Fox Claw. God, hadn't Fox Claw done exactly what he himself had once done—killed a woman and a child in war? Ah, he knew him, he knew him too well. Fox Claw was the man he had always hunted. Their trails had crossed and recrossed—how many times?

The hunt took on meaning for Curtis, a meaning that had only been latent before. He could not explain it, but he felt it. His life was somehow bound up with that of the man he hunted. It was a strange kinship that he felt, but it was kinship.

He rode on, ignoring the cold wind that blew in his face.

The day came, as it had to come.

Jim, the Tonk scout, rode in to rejoin the column

after an absence of nearly four hours. Jim had gone out before daybreak to have a look around. He had a big grin on his old face now. Curtis knew without asking that he had found Fox Claw.

Curtis lifted his hand and halted the colomn.

"Well, Jim?"

Jim nodded. "We catch him now maybe. God damn."

"How far away is he?"

Jim frowned. He wasn't much good at estimating distances. A mile to Jim might be almost anything.

Curtis rephrased his question. "How long will it take to get there?"

"Take hour maybe. Depend on how fast you ride."

"Any cover?"

"Land is pretty flat, I think. God damn. That bad Indian is back of a small hill. One other Indian with him."

"Only one?"

"I say one." Jim shrugged. "There only one."

"No cover at all for us?"

"Close to hill on this side. There is dry stream. Room for some."

Curtis nodded. Quickly, he thought the situation through. He had a good chance to get his man. He couldn't afford any mistakes now.

"Matt."

"Sir?"

"Pick six men. Good shots. Make sure they have good horses. Check their provisions."

"Right."

"Lieutenant Pease."

"Sir?"

"Captain Irvine and I will take Jim and six men. We'll try to make that dry stream bed without being seen. That should be close enough so that we can get him before he can run. You are to hold the main body of men here. If you hear shooting, come after us. You may be too far away to hear the shots; I don't know. If you don't hear any shooting after two hours, put one of the Tonks on our trail and follow us. If we become separated, return here before nightfall and make camp. We'll get back to you sooner or later. Clear?"

"Yes, sir." Lieutenant Pease looked disappointed.

"Sorry to leave you behind," Curtis said. "We don't have a chance of getting the whole company up there without being spotted. This is the only way." Curtis smiled. "You know *I'd* rather take the whole company, don't you?"

Pease managed a grin. "Right, sir. You can count on me. Good luck."

Curtis turned in his saddle. "Ready, Matt?"

"All set."

"Let's go. Jim, lead the way. Use all the cover you can find. No talking. No noise you can avoid."

"God damn," Jim said.

The party of nine men started for the dry stream bed, riding at a fast walk.

They made it without incident.

Dismounted in the dry stream cut, Curtis could see the low hill rising out of the plains before him. It was less than half a mile away. It was impossible to tell whether or not Fox Claw was still there.

There was no cover between them and the hill.

"I don't like it," Matt whispered. "Too far."

Curtis studied the hill, considering. "Those two men are not fools," he said quietly. "One of them is probably keeping a lookout from that hill. If we come galloping out of this draw they'll hightail it. We might be able to catch them. I don't know."

"It's a chance," Matt said. "We have to take it, I guess. But I still don't like it."

"Neither do I." Curtis stared at the hill. He could see no sign of life. "If Fox Claw is still there, I don't want to miss him."

"Him there," Jim said confidently. "God damn."

Curtis turned to his Tonk scout. He felt a quick excitement growing in him. "Jim, would you ride out there with me? Just the two of us?"

Jim shrugged. He was not enthusiastic.

Neither was Matt Irvine. "That's no good," he said bluntly. "They'll see you coming."

"Exactly," Curtis said.

"They'll just pick you off like sitting ducks. Where does that get us?"

"Matt, suppose Jim and I ride out there with a white flag? Nobody else—just the two of us. Fox Claw won't know that the rest of you are waiting in this draw. Two men can't scare him very much. If he sees the white flag, maybe he'll talk."

"Maybe he'll blow your head off. He's a killer."

"But maybe he'll give himself up if I talk to him. What else can we do? If we all ride out there, even with a white flag, he'll run. He might run just from the two of us. But he *might* listen."

"No. You're taking a crazy chance."

Curtis looked at him. "If you have a better plan, let's hear it."

Matt hesitated. There was no other plan that had a chance of success. "Let me go," he said.

"No. This is my job."

Curtis had his mind made up. From the moment he had thought of trying to talk to Fox Claw the idea had been irresistible to him. Wild horses couldn't have stopped him now.

He took his revolver out of his holster, checked it, and put it in the left pocket of his heavy coat. He picked up a damp stick from the stream bed and tied a moderately clean white handkerchief to one end of it. He told Jim to take his carbine, but ordered him to keep it under his blanket, out of sight.

"You're wasting your time, sir," Matt protested. "He'll never come in. You're risking your life for nothing."

Curtis smiled. "Don't look so anxious, Matt. I'm not going up before a firing squad. I can use that .44, if it comes to that. Jim's a good shot. There are only two of them."

"But—"

Curtis stopped smiling. "But nothing. The decision is made. Here are your orders. Keep your men mounted, here in the draw. If there is any shooting, or any trouble, then come fast. If Jim and I come hightailing it back at a gallop, ride out to meet us and be ready to fight. Otherwise, stay put. Got that?"

"Yes, sir." Matt took a deep breath. "Good luck. We'll be ready."

"All set, Jim?"

Jim nodded, his old seamed face impassive. Jim hated the Comanches like poison. "God damn," he said.

The two men rode out from the cover of the dry stream cut.

Jim led the way, his small hunched figure almost dwarfed by the big cavalry horse he rode. Curtis followed him closely. His right hand, gripping the reins, held the white flag aloft. His left hand rested on the warm butt of the .44 in his coat pocket.

It was a dismal gray day. The wind had turned much colder. The clouds were very low in the sky, dark-edged and heavy. The land looked dull and barren. It felt like a norther was on the way.

The hooves of the two horses clicked sharply against the cold earth. They hadn't ridden a hundred yards before Curtis felt utterly alone. He and Jim might have been the only men left in all the world. The wind keened around him, plucking at his coat. The wind was definitely shifting around to the north. A north wind always sounded more lonely than any other kind.

It seemed to take forever for them to close the distance that separated them from the hill. Curtis had plenty of time to think about what he was doing—too much time.

Fox Claw was waiting there ahead of him. He was probably caught in the sights of Fox Claw's rifle already. But Curtis could not hate Fox Claw. He would kill him if he had to, yes, or Fox Claw would kill Curtis. But he did not hate the man. He did not admire him or envy him, not quite. But he was conscious of him, aware of him as a human being.

Curtis knew that he was no better than the man he hunted. He hope he was no worse. He thought that he was different. That was all.

Fox Claw was a savage. Very well; accept that. He,

Curtis, was not a savage, was he? *Was he?* Did all civilization, all thought, having nothing better to offer than this—you kill me and I'll kill you?

He *had* to talk to Fox Claw.

He had to try.

If he failed, it would not be his failure.

They rode straight at the small rise. It really couldn't be called a hill, but it was impossible to see the other side of it. It was farther away than it looked.

Just before they reached it, Curtis reined in his horse.

"Hold on, Jim," he said. "We'll sit here a spell. Give him a chance to look us over if he's still there."

"God damn," Jim said with feeling.

Curtis had trouble holding his horse still. Perhaps the animal sensed the nervousness of his rider. Curtis waved the white handkerchief slowly back and forth. The wind whipped it straight out from the stick and it flapped loudly.

The seconds became minutes. They were very long minutes. It was possible that Fox Claw had flown the coop, but in his heart Curtis did not doubt that two rifles were trained right on his chest. He looked closely but he could still see nothing.

He waited. There was nothing else he could do. He did not regret his decision, but he wished that the whole thing were over. He did not particularly fancy being a target.

He was very cold.

He began to feel foolish, and Jim's unspoken thoughts didn't help matters any.

He kept waving the handkerchief on a stick.

"Come on, damn you," he whispered. "One more minute and I'm going to ride over that hill and crack this stick over your thick skull."

Then he heard the horse coming.

Fox Claw rode over the rise.

Curtis felt his heart stop, then start again. Moving very slowly and carefully, he passed the white flag over to Jim. He raised his right hand, palm outward.

Fox Claw made no sigh. He just rode to them and stopped. He had an old rifle cradled in his arm. He neither smiled nor frowned. He stared at Curtis. His horse twitched his ears, pointing.

Curtis stared at him. His nervousness was gone; he was steady. Fox Claw looked old, and he looked tired. He was bone-thin and dirty. His long black hair was matted and tangled. His face was a bone mask creased with dirty lines; the high cheekbones almost punched through the tight skin. The once powerful neck was scrawny. Only his eyes seemed alive. They burned like coals of black ice in their sunken sockets.

"I am Colonel Curtis," Curtis said.

Fox Claw said nothing. He did not react in any way.

"Do you understand English?"

Fox Claw stared at him. It was like talking to a rock.

Curtis tried. "I have come to ask you to give yourself up," he said. "There is no chance for you if you do not surrender. If you will come in, I will do everything I can to help you. That is a promise. I will try to be your friend. There has been enough killing."

The cold wind sighed across the plains.

Fox Claw said nothing.

"Jim. Does he get what I am saying to him?"

Jim shrugged.

"Tell him exactly what I said."

"Him not listen to Tonkawa."

"Tell him anyway. *Exactly* what I said. Nothing else."

Jim tried, though his heart wasn't in it. He spoke Comanche slowly, with difficulty, as though the words hurt his mouth. He made signs as he talked. He almost dropped the white handkerchief as he gestured.

Fox Claw did not even look at the Tonk. He kept his eyes fixed on Curtis.

Curtis took a deep breath. "Tell him that if he does not come in now he will get no other chance," he said flatly. "I will have no choice except to hunt him down and kill him."

Jim relayed this message with considerably more enthusiasm.

Fox Claw waited a long minute. Then, carefully and deliberately, he spat on the ground.

Curtis gripped the .44 in his coat pocket. He swore to

himself. He could not talk to this man. He could not communicate with him. He could not touch him. All of his fancy thoughts were so much air in the gulf that separated them. There were no words for what he wanted to say. Not in English. Not in Comanche. There was no bridge. No amount of determination on his part could change that fact.

Still, Fox Claw had honored the white flag. He had held his fire. That was something.

"Tell him good-bye," Curtis said.

Jim did so, shortly.

Fox Claw smiled faintly and made no other sign.

"Let's go, Jim. Keep the flag up in the air. ride back ahead of me."

He let Jim get a slight lead. Then he nodded to Fox Claw, wheeled his horse around, and followed. His hand was sweating on the butt of the .44 in his pocket. His back felt naked.

There was no shot.

His back knew it when Fox Claw was no longer there. Curtis twisted in his saddle and looked behind him. The rise was empty and barren under the cold gray sky.

He followed Jim into the draw where Matt was waiting with the mounted men. His body was clammy with sweat under his coat. Matt grinned broadly at him.

Curtis wasted no time.

"All right, gentlemen," he said. "He's there. He won't come in. Let's go and get him."

The soldiers charged through the darkening November day.

It was a ragged charge, almost an amateur's charge. Even as he rode, Curtis was faintly surprised at himself for making it. They were nine men riding in an exposed line at a good defensive position.

He spurred his horse. He wanted to get it over with, end it once and for all. Despite himself, he was stung by Fox Claw's insulting refusal to talk. And he had hunted this man for a very long time. He wanted him.

He was ready to kill.

He was the hunter. He wanted to punish his prey for

his cunning in eluding him, punish him for all the cold nights and long days.

Curtis was the master. He wanted to prove it with a bullet.

They rode at a full gallop. The cold wind cut their faces. They covered the distance to the rise in a few short minutes. There was no resistance, no sign of life.

They topped the rise, sabers glinting dully and guns at the ready. They charged down the other side before they could come to a halt.

Fox Claw wasn't there.

The Indians had vanished.

The only mark they had left on the earth was a small smokeless fire of buffalo dung in the hollow. The fire was still burning.

Curtis jerked his horse back to the top of the rise. He shielded his eyes out of habit; there was no sun. The wind whipped at his coat. His gray eyes searched the land. There was nothing to see. There was no hiding place visible except the cut where Matt and his men had waited. The plains seemed utterly deserted. There was only dead brown grass shivering in the wind. The leaden sky was very close, hugging the earth.

He rode back to the little fire.

"Jim. Can you find the trail?"

The old Tonk dismounted and began to walk around the fire in widening circles. He looked like a blanketed gargoyle, crouching down with his nose to the ground like an animal. He could not hurry. It was slow work.

The wind rose and the sky grew still darker.

Jim finally straightened up. "Here," he said. "This way. Two horses."

"Matt. They don't have much of a lead on us. What do you think?"

Matt squinted. "Storm coming up, I reckon. We might give it a try. I don't know."

Curtis only hesitated a moment. He wanted Fox Claw. If they had a chance at him they had to take it. They weren't much worse off than they would have been if he had not tried to talk to Fox Claw. A minute or two further behind perhaps.

"Lead the way, Jim. As fast as you can."

"Big storm," the Tonk said.

"Yes. Lead the way."

Jim shrugged and mounted his horse. He started off at a fast walk, his eyes scanning the ground. The soldiers fell in behind him.

Within half an hour Curtis knew it was hopeless. They could not track the Indians and narrow the gap at the same time. Their only chance was to spot them somehow and make a run for them. He said nothing.

The nine men rode on.

After about an hour the wind stopped suddenly. The footfalls of the horses sounded as loud as shots in the hushed air. It got very cold, and very still. The sky turned black over their heads.

The rain started.

It was only an icy drizzle at first, but then it began to come down hard. There was no lightning. The wind came up again, straight out of the north. It blew the rain in cold gray sheets across the flatlands. The hooves of the horses began to splash in thin snakes of running water.

It was hard to see anything. The trail was washed out completely.

Very shortly, Curtis knew, it would be pitch dark.

The rain was freezing cold. It had sleet in it.

Curtis gave up. He could not risk the safety of his command through sheer stubborn idiocy. He should have turned back before. But he hadn't been sure about the storm. Jim was always very quick with his predictions about the weather, and he was dead wrong as often as he was right.

There was no question about it now. They were smack in the middle of a blue norther. Indians or no Indians, a blue norther was nothing to fool around with. The temperature was dropping very fast. He could actually feel it getting colder by the minute.

Winter had come to the Staked Plains.

He rode up next to Jim and leaned over in his saddle. "Jim!" He had to yell to make himself heard. "Take us back to camp, where I told Lieutenant Pease to wait. A bottle of whiskey if we make it before dark!"

"God damn," said Jim.

Jim swung them around in a hurry and started off at a fast trot. Curtis was almost completely disoriented in the storm, but he trusted Jim's sense of direction. The Tonk had gotten him out of tough places before. Jim always seemed to know where he was going, even if he didn't have much of a notion about how long it might take to get there. If there was whiskey at the end of the trail, he would get there with reasonable speed. If there was a full bottle, he would get there fast if he had to swim rivers and climb mountains.

Curtis was soaking wet and he did not have a slicker with him. The icy water ran down the back of his neck when it overflowed his hat. The wind cut through him like a knife and his hand was numb on the reins. He remembered the story of a cowboy who had gotten himself caught in a blue norther. The cowboy had been mounted on a fast horse, and he had tried to outride the norther to the bunkhouse. The story was that the cowboy had just been able to keep even with the storm, and when he had pulled into the ranch the hindquarters of his horse had been frozen solid.

The story didn't seem very funny now.

He did not shiver. His body had no feeling left in it. He just held on and followed Jim through the rain.

Numbly, he thought of old Fox Claw, out here somewhere riding through this same storm. (Old? He wasn't as old as Curtis, probably. But he seemed old, old as the rocks and the sand and the wind. And he was thin; the man had no meat on him. He would feel the cold.) Why didn't Fox Claw quit? What was it that kept him going when he had no chance at all?

The cold fury of the storm cut his plans down to size. What did it matter? He almost hoped that Fox Claw would get away.

He bent his dripping head against the bite of the north wind.

Run, you fool! he thought. *Run and keep on running. Run and don't come back.*

But he knew that Fox Claw would not run forever.

The winter would be long, but not long enough.

The time for killing would come again.

Fox Claw

There were milky crusts of new ice on the water holes beneath the gray waste of the sky. Small drifts of clean white snow lay in the sheltered hollows. The land was hard now, hard and frozen, and the air was crystal clear and very still.

The wind did not blow in February on the Staked Plains.

In all the world nothing moved. Fox Claw stood in the terrible cold, his black eyes fever-bright in the sockets of his skull. He wanted a fire. He remembered fire. But he was too wise for that, too wise with a cunning that was beyond all thinking. The smoke would rise high in the still air. It could be seen for miles.

He could not see the soldiers this day. At least, he could not remember having seen them. But he knew that the soldiers would be watching for him. They were always there.

Fox Claw had almost lost the sense of time. It seemed to him that the winter had been very long. Still, one day was much like another. It was hard to tell. He could hardly remember a time when he had not been watching the dark blue columns winding like strange cold-weather snakes across the frozen land. Back and forth crawled the blue snakes. They went from the cap rock west to the Pecos and north to the Canadian. Sometimes, when the storms were bad, they vanished for a few days. But they always returned. The soldiers had come to stay. The snakes were hungry.

Fox Claw stood very still in the cold. His eyes were open but he was not really looking at anything. He was just standing there, and that was all.

He had no plan of action. He had no hope, and no

fear. He existed with only one conscious purpose. He wanted to live until the cycle of his life was complete. He did not know when that would be; he knew only that he would recognize it when the time came. Something deep within him kept him going, kept him alive. He had survived, and that was everything.

He could not remember when he had eaten last. He did not want to remember. He did remember leaving most of his horses with Broken Bow. He remembered killing one for food. That had been long ago. That had been at the beginning of winter, after he had lost the white-eyed soldier in the storm. Now even Watcher was thin and his body was covered with sores. It hurt Fox Claw to look at him.

There had been no raids for many, many days. That too was finished. He was too tired to raid, too tired to think. Dies Young was his only warrior. Long ago, River Smoke had run away. The young man was wise to go. There was nothing left for him with Fox Claw and Dies Young.

Dies Young had lost his fat. It was hard to remember him as a big man. His skin hung on him now in folds like empty parfleche bags. His eyes were dead. Dies Young coughed in his sleep and there was often blood on his mouth.

The earth began to move before Fox Claw's eyes. It tilted, very slowly, until he seemed to be looking at it sideways. It started to spin, still slowly, as though something were trying to hold it back. It took a long time to go all the way around. It stopped, just for a moment. It started around again.

Fox Claw blinked his eyes and the earth steadied. He was very cold, like a corpse. His buffalo robe was cracked and peeling. He could not feel his feet. He had not been able to get his moccasins off the last time he had tried. There was a smooth ball of ice in his belly. It dripped upwards, into his chest. That was strange. He could feel the cold drops hitting one by one.

He knew that he should move. He should not stand still. If he did, he would die. It was not time to die yet.

He tried to think of where he might go. He could not think.

It was easier to remember.

It was curious. He could not remember what had happened yesterday, or even this morning. But he could remember what had happened long ago. He could feel the way it had been, exact in every detail.

He remembered how warm the great tepees had been in the old days, in that other life. He missed the warmth. He missed the summer sun that he would not see again, but the warmth of the tepees had been good too. February was the month for sleeping. There was nothing else to do then. He could feel the clean furs against his skin. They had been warm and cozy, like a nest. His mother had kept the fire going in precisely the right way, pushing in one stick at a time. There had been strange dreams when he woke up and dozed off again. Good dreams, mostly. And there had been good hot stews that burned in his throat. How hot those stews had been! It had been pleasant to lie in his furs and smell the food bubbling in the cooking pot and think of Warm Wind.

It was all gone now.

He was very cold.

He wished that he dared to build a fire.

The cold was terrible. He could think of nothing else. There must be warmth somewhere. There must be a place that he could go, a place that was still warm. He tried to remember. Something warm and soft—

Something that might welcome him, be glad to see him. In all the world, something, somewhere. . . .

Little Cousin. He remembered his dog. He had not seen Little Cousin for a long time. He had left him with Broken Bow. He could almost feel the small heart beating against the soft warm fur.

Little Cousin was a part of summer.

He would go back to the warmth of summer.

His body moved. He had to force it to move, think about it carefully as though his body no longer belonged to him. It didn't work very well. It was too cold. He walked stiff-legged, clumsily, like a very old man.

He found Dies Young asleep in a hollow he had

managed to scoop out under a shallow ledge of rock. He pulled at Dies Young's shoulder. Dies Young opened his lifeless eyes and looked at him without interest.

Fox Claw made words in his mouth. It was hard; his throat was raw and dry. "I want to find Broken Bow," he said. "It may be that he has food."

Dies Young did not move. He closed his eyes again. He might have gone back to sleep; Fox Claw could not tell. Fox Claw did not disturb him again. It was too much of an effort. He had said what he had to say. If Dies Young wished to come he would come. If not, he would stay.

Fox Claw called Watcher to him. He rubbed his cold ears. Watcher was very thin; Fox Claw could hear his breathing. He wondered if Watcher remembered the summer. He wondered if Watcher remembered the warm grass that dried in the sun.

He pulled himself up on Watcher's back. Watcher had the sick smell in him.

He turned and looked back. Dies Young had come out of his hollow. He was moving, getting his horse ready. Dies Young was coming with him. Dimly, Fox Claw was glad. He did not want to be alone.

Dies Young mounted. He climbed on his horse with difficulty, but once he was there he seemed better. As always, he became a part of his horse. His cracked lips broke into a kind of smile. He could still ride.

Side by side they rode out of nowhere, looking for the camp of Broken Bow.

All that day they rode through silence. There was nothing to eat. There was no shelter from the cold. Twice Fox Claw lost consciousness, but he did not fall. Each time when he came to himself again Watcher was still picking his way over the frozen land as though nothing had happened.

The two men did not speak. It took strength to talk.

They saw no soldiers.

The day turned into night. It was a slow change and it made no difference. The night was a little colder, and that was all. It was so still that Fox Claw could hear every labored breath that Watcher took.

Somehow, the night ended. The sky turned gray again.

They were more dead than alive when they reached the camp of Broken Bow.

At first, Fox Claw did not realize that anything was wrong. He was so tired that his numb brain could not understand what his eyes saw. The tepees were still standing, still intact. The camp was neat and orderly. He wondered where the people were. There was no sound of greeting. The place was as still as death.

He looked for a fire. He had to have a fire.

He saw the bodies then. For just a moment, they looked almost as though they were sleeping. But they were too still. And they were not in the tepees. They were out on the frozen ground. . . .

Fox Claw jerked himself back to awareness. He stared around him. He forced himself to think, to comprehend.

The silent camp told its own story. The winter had given time to Broken Bow, but it had not saved him. In the end, Broken Bow had had to fight.

The old man had pitched his tepees against the cold. Yes, and he had allowed his women to build fires. He knew the danger in building fires, but Fox Claw understood. There comes a time when danger no longer matters. There comes a time when the cold is all there is. There comes a time when all an old man can see are hungry children whose bodies freeze in the long nights.

Some of the tepees had bullet holes in them, but they had not been burned. The camp was undisturbed, as though the little band had just gone away for awhile.

The fight must have been short.

Fox Claw dismounted stiffly. He could hardly walk. He sniffed the air. There was no smell of death. The cold had kept the bodies clean. There were no birds in the empty gray sky.

He walked from body to body, looking at them. He felt oddly detached. He reacted very little to what he saw. He had known that the army would catch Broken Bow and it had caught him. He was sorry that it had happened but it could not touch him deeply. It was all like something that had taken place a long time ago. He found Broken

Bow. The old man had three bullet holes in his frozen body. He looked at three of the women lying together in a heap. They had been cut by sabers. He did not see River Smoke. There were many others who were missing. He saw no dead children.

The soldiers had taken some prisoners. Perhaps that was good.

Fox Claw kept walking. He was as cold as ice.

He found Little Cousin.

He looked down at the small body. Something inside of him collapsed, something that he had not known was still there. It was a final barrier and when it gave way he had nothing left. The cold hollow emptiness inside him was filled by a red surge of madness. He could not stand against it. He fell down with a mindless cry.

The red madness turned black. Then for a long time there was nothing.

He came back to his senses on the cold ground. Numbly, he reached out and tried to cradle the thin frozen body of Little Cousin in his arms. He remembered the warmth. He wanted it.

But there was no warmth now. The ice-matted fur was stiff and hard. The cold white teeth were bared in an ugly snarl.

Little Cousin had failed him.

He lurched to his feet. He threw the dog's body from him. It hit solidly, like a rock.

The madness filled him, choking him. He ran from empty tepee to empty tepee, searching for food like an animal. There was no food. There was not even a scrap of pemmican. The tepees had been picked clean long before the soldiers had come.

There might still be a dead horse near the camp. He ran through the flat brown grass. He could not feel his feet. He ran hard with a force that stained his moccasins with black spots of greasy blood. There were no horses. The band of Broken Bow had been caught on foot. The soldiers had taken all the horses away with them.

He stopped running. He stood still, his chest heaving. The cold air hurt his lungs. He saw Dies Young. Dies

Young had not dismounted. He was still sitting quietly on his horse, watching him through cloudy eyes.

"Build a fire," Fox Claw said. His voice was like a sharp stone in his throat. He pointed. "Build it there—in front of that tepee where there is still wood."

For a long moment Dies Young did nothing. Then he dismounted slowly. His body was bent almost double by a spasm of coughing. He stepped painfully into the tepee to cut some dry shavings from a tepee pole. He asked no questions. They both knew that they would die without a fire.

Fox Claw unsheathed his knife. He squatted down before the rigid body of the dog. There was nothing else to eat.

He cut off the head first. It took a long time. He was not strong and the flesh was hard all the way through. He threw the head away. He sliced the stiff hide along the backbone. He ripped it off with numb fingers. He tore his nails until they bled but he felt nothing.

He frowned. There was not much meat on Little Cousin. He had lost his fat. He hacked the meat into two parts.

Dies Young's fire burned badly. The cold brush wood was thin and black. As it thawed it dripped beads of dark water into the hissing tongues of yellow flame. There was a lot of greasy smoke.

Fox Claw went over to help. They nursed the fire, willing it to life. They kept it going with dry shavings until the wet wood caught. It took them more than an hour to get real heat. They stayed very close to the fire, almost burning themselves. They drank the heat.

They waited until they had good red coals. Then they cut forked sticks and wedged the meat into the points until it would hold. Carefully, they arranged the meat just over the coals.

The meat thawed quickly.

It began to cook. The meat sputtered and dripped. It sizzled, dropping grease into the coals. It smelled good, good and hot. It turned brown, then black.

Fox Claw waited as long as he could. Then he pulled the meat from the coals. He bit into it. It was so hot it burned his mouth. It was raw on the inside. It tasted rich and sweet. It was easier to chew than buffalo meat.

He ate it all. When he was through he sat by the fire and sucked the pasty marrow out of the bones.

When he had finished his portion, Dies Young got to his feet. He said nothing. He went into the tepee and carefully built another small fire in the depression under the smoke hole, using the hot coals to get it going. He slowly dragged a supply of damp wood inside and arranged it around the fire where it would dry. He placed his rifle down by the side of the raised platform bed. He got up on the bed, fully clothed, and pulled his dirty buffalo robe over his body. He coughed once, wiped his mouth with his hand, and then lay very still. His eyes were open.

Fox Claw stayed outside. He was warm enough and some feeling had come back to his hands. He stared into the little fire. His head was clear, clearer than it had been for many days, but he felt a sickness growing inside him.

He had gone too long without food. The meat stuck in his belly like knots of hard wood. He started to sweat. He didn't think he could keep the food down.

He tried. He clenched his fists and clamped his teeth together. He rocked gently back and forth by the fire. He told himself that he needed the strength the meat would give him.

But it hurt. A wave of nausea swept over him.

He stood up, despising himself. He walked away from the tepee and knelt down on the cold earth. He was sick and shaking. He wanted to lose the meat but it wouldn't come up.

He stuck two fingers of his right hand far down his throat. He kept them there until he gagged. Nothing came up. He tried again, sweating. This time he was violently sick. His stomach heaved convulsively long after it was empty. He could not get back to his feet when he was through.

Shaking, he crawled back to the fire. He curled his body around it, seeking warmth. He closed his eyes.

Perhaps, he thought, it was just as well. He would have kept the meat in him if he could; he needed it. But he knew that it was wrong. It was not that he had eaten his dog. Little Cousin was dead; he would not mind. But The People did not eat dogs. The dog was forbidden to them.

Fox Claw smiled a little. It seemed that he could not break the laws of his people even when he tried. It might be that it was better that way.

He dozed. The fire died and went out. It was getting dark. He was cold again.

He managed to get up. He was light-headed but he could stand. He took a deep breath, hating the pain in his chest. He looked around him.

Nothing was left. The camp was dead and the warriors were gone. The land that had been his home was cold and alien. He had done his best. He could do no more. The ritual cycle was almost complete. He had very little time left.

He pulled back the flap and stepped into the tepee. It felt very hot inside and the air was stale. The fire under the smoke hole had died down to a bed of glowing orange coals.

He looked at Dies Young. His eyes were open. There was sick sweat glistening on his lined face.

"How is it with you?" he asked.

"I am well," Dies Young said. His words were slow. "It is warm here."

"We have ridden much together, we two."

"Yes."

"You will not ride again, I think."

"No. I will stay."

"Is it your wish that I should kill your horse for you?"

"No. He has given much to me, that horse. I am not hungry now. That food would not help me."

"Is it your wish that I should stay with you?"

Dies Young closed his eyes. His voice was very weak. "It is time for each man to go alone. Even brothers."

"It will not be for long.

"No. Not for long now."

There was nothing more to be said. Fox Claw put some more wood on the coals. He went outside and gathered up the rest of the wood and piled it by the fire. Then he went out and closed the tepee flap behind him.

He caught Dies Young's horse and tied him outside the tepee. He tethered him loosely so that he could pull himself free in time. He started to saddle him, but he changed his mind and left the saddle on the frozen ground.

Fox Claw picked up his rifle and checked it over. It was cold and scarred but it would still shoot. It would not fail him. He tried to whistle for Watcher but his lips were too cracked and stiff. He walked over and caught his horse. It was not difficult; there had been little food for his horse, and Watcher was weak. He mounted. Watcher's breath came hard. Fox Claw leaned forward and warmed Watcher's cold ears with his hands.

Fox Claw took nothing that he did not need. He wanted to make it as easy for Watcher as he could. He even left his buffalo robe on the ground. He could stand one night without it.

He whispered into Watcher's ear. "Come, my horse," he said. "See! The clouds are torn this night. There are stars to light our way. It is not far that we will ride, you and I."

Watcher whinnied softly.

They rode out of the dead camp of Broken Bow.

It was very cold and very still. Fox Claw did not feel the bitter cold, not at first. The world was hushed and empty, as though life itself was frozen. Fox Claw welcomed the silence.

They rode on into the night.

Fox Claw was strangely content. He was alone now, truly alone. Even Dies Young was gone. He had always known that it would end this way. Years ago, when the world was young, he had set out on that first vision quest alone. He had become a man alone. That was the way. Now he would ride his last trail alone. He had made the choice. He did not regret it.

Much later, in the stillness and the cold, he looked up.

He saw the silver moon gliding through a canyon in the clouds.

Mother Moon was watching.

* * *

Fox Claw found the camp of the soldiers just after daybreak.

He had known where the army would be. For long months he had observed the dark columns marching like ants back and forth across the Staked Plains. He knew their habits, and he knew the possibilities of the country. He knew their sleeping places, every one of them.

He looked at the camp. It might have been the camp of the soldiers who had attacked Broken Bow. It might not. There was no way to tell. The prisoners and the horses would have been taken to some safer place. It made no difference to Fox Claw. One group of soldiers was the same as another.

He was cold now, cold with the dawn light that gave no warmth. He had ridden all night without a robe. He had no feeling in his hands and feet. The icy dripping in his chest hurt him. His mind was slow and cold, like a turtle caught in the winter snows.

The camp in front of him was very different from the camp he had left the night before. There were many tents, and they were little sharp-cornered things that hugged the earth. The *Taibos* were careless. They had nothing to fear. They talked in loud ugly voices; he could hear their gabble distinctly from the rock shadow where Watcher stood. He could smell warm fragrant cooking smells in the air. There was much food here, and much coffee. Coffee was one good thing the white men had. He could smell the coffee very clearly. Fox Claw liked coffee. He liked it hot, very hot, with much sugar in it.

He could see the army horses. So many horses. . . .

The *Taibos* were very rich.

Fox Claw swayed and almost fell. He hated the weakness that was in him. A warrior should be strong. He did not have much time left.

He rubbed his hands together, trying to warm them. His hands were rough and hard, like a woman's. At first, he could feel nothing. Then, slowly, his hands returned to him. He could feel his rifle and his knife.

He was ready.

He rode out of the rock shadow.

The light was good but they did not see him. He

made no effort at concealment. He rode straight toward the camp at a steady pace.

He experienced again that strange splitting sensation as though he had become two men. One of him was on Watcher's back with the rifle cold in his hands. The other Fox Claw looked down from the sky. He saw himself clearly, a small black figure in the immensity of the land, riding slowly toward the neat white lines of the tents. It was warmer in the sky. The clouds were edged with the color of the wild rose. The sun would shine this day—

One of the sentries spotted him.

Fox Claw heard the cry of alarm. It sounded very close. He heard the cold crack of the first rifle. He heard the bullet when it thudded into the frozen earth ahead of him.

It was possible, he thought, that the first shot had been intended to miss. The soldiers did that sometimes, as a warning. He smiled.

He leaned forward. "Come, my horse," he whispered. "One last time."

Watcher tossed his head and broke into an unsteady gallop. Fox Claw dropped to the side of his horse, clutching him around the neck with his left arm while his right hand held his rifle at the ready. Watcher ran like the veteran he was. He gave it all he had.

Above the drumming of Watcher's hooves on the cold ground Fox Claw heard the shouts of the soldiers and the sharp cracks of rifles. He ignored them.

He was in the camp before they had a chance to be ready for him. Fox Claw was very calm. He picked his man carefully. Watcher ran straight at the soldier and Fox Claw fired. The man stumbled and Watcher went right over him.

He was through the camp and out the other side. He was surprised that he had not been hit. He heard bullets whining around his ears.

It came to him, as in a dream, that he might get away. He pushed the thought aside. He had no place left to go.

He turned Watcher in a great circle and started back for the camp. Watcher faltered but kept going.

This time the soldiers were ready. They had managed to form a ragged line. He thought he saw the tall man who had once spoken to him under the white flag. He did not remember his name.

Fox Claw charged again.

He saw the tiny flames that darted from the muzzles of the rifles. He heard the steady rattle of the firing.

He felt the bullets that hit Watcher. There were many of them. He felt them as sharply as though they had shocked his own flesh. Watcher stumbled and went down, hard. Fox Claw threw himself clear.

Fox Claw got to his feet. He threw his useless rifle away and pulled his knife.

He stood up straight. He ran at the soldiers, his knife in his hand.

The guns kept firing.

Something hit his shoulder. It did not hurt but it knocked him down. He was surprised that there was no pain. He got up again and took four steps. Something struck his chest. He fell and found that he could not get up.

He crawled at the soldiers, gripping his knife tightly.

He saw a wall of fire in front of him. It was very bright. It burned his eyes. He closed his eyes and there was nothing.

He opened his eyes a moment later. It was all gone. Everything was gone. There were no soldiers. There was no wall of fire. There was no sound.

He looked down. The dead brown grass beneath him had changed. It was green, green and thick and fresh. It was warm to lie on, warm as from the summer sun. He could smell it. It had life in it.

He raised his head. There was a light in the air, a glow of silver-gold. He knew that light. Once before he had seen it. He had never forgotten.

He turned his head, slowly.

He saw him. For the second time, he saw him. He smiled. It was given to few men to see him twice.

The great bull buffalo stood in the tall grass. He was very close. He was exactly the same. He had not aged in all the years since Spirit Hill. (Had Buffalo Tongue seen him before he died? Fox Claw was sure that he had. That too was a good thing.) The buffalo's powerful shoulders and hump were shaggy with black-brown hair. There were flies buzzing on his flanks where the hair had fallen out to leave patches of naked hide. His sharp white horns glinted in the sun. He stood quite still except for the twitching of his tufted tail.

The buffalo looked at Fox Claw with weak, waiting eyes.

Fox Claw struggled to his feet. He could not feel anything. He took one step toward the buffalo.

The buffalo turned and walked away, slowly.

"No," whispered Fox Claw.

He tried to follow him but something was wrong with his legs. They would not hold him. He fell.

He dropped his knife and pulled himself hand over hand through the soft green grass. He could tell when he reached the place where the buffalo had stood. The grass was flattened from his weight. The grass stems were wet and broken in the silver-gold light. The smell of buffalo was very strong. It was a good smell.

He tried but he could not go any further. There was no strength left in his body.

He lifted his head.

The buffalo was coming back for him.

Fox Claw's heart sang.

He stretched out his right hand, reaching.

He did not feel the bullets. They were not real.

They were not in Fox Claw's world.

Curtis

The flag and guidon of A Company hung limply in the still air. The column moved slowly across the flat brown land. Behind the soldiers, following them step by cold step, a final silence flowed in over the dead earth of the Staked Plains.

It was more like a funeral procession than anything else, Curtis thought. They even had a couple of bodies to complete the illusion. The body of the soldier Fox Claw had killed was in one supply wagon. Fox Claw's body was in another, wrapped in a sheet of stiff gray canvas.

The army's job was done. The column was going back to Fort Wade, but the men were quiet and subdued. It wasn't that there was any feeling of regret, as far as Curtis knew. The men were just too tired to talk.

Curtis held himself straight in his saddle. It took a real effort on his part, but it was important to him. He was damned if he would ride back to Wade looking like a beaten man.

He had no feeling of elation. He had won his fight with the Indians, but he had always known that he would win that fight. The final outcome had never been in doubt.

He was certainly not sorry that he had won. He had done his job, and more than that. He had given Fox Claw a chance. He was proud of that. Fox Claw was what he was; he would not have welcomed pity.

But Curtis was anything but happy. He knew his tail was dragging, whether it showed or not. It went deeper than Fox Claw, deeper than surface victory or defeat. He felt as though he were riding from one world to another. He knew the world he was leaving. He did not know the world that still lay before him.

He was too tired to think about it.

He did not look at the land as he rode. He did not want to see it. He pulled his heavy coat more closely around him. The sun was shining, but he was cold. He kept his eyes fixed on the dirty blanket on Jim's back, following wherever it led.

Sometimes, it was good not to lead.

It was easier to follow, to abdicate responsibility for a time. It was pleasant to have a guide from one world to another, even a guide in a dirty blanket.

He was glad when the column stopped for lunch. He was in no hurry to get where he was going.

Curtis ate his beans from a tin plate. He didn't relish beans at the best of times, and these seemed more tasteless than usual. The coffee, though, was good and hot. He drank three cups.

He was too tired for the coffee to have much effect on

him. He almost dozed off in the thin sunlight. Then he looked up and saw a knot of his men gathered around the wagon that held Fox Claw's body. He got stiffly to his feet and walked over to them.

They had unrolled the heavy canvas. Fox Claw was lying in the dirt, face up. Sergeant Fitzgerald was trying to cut off Fox Claw's moccasins with a knife.

"Having trouble, sergeant?"

Fitzgerald straightened up, his red face sweating in the cold. "Damn me if I can get 'em off, sir. They're stuck to his feet with blood. I thought they might make a bit of a souvenir, if you know what I mean, sir." He paused, looking at Curtis. "You didn't want them for yourself, sir?"

"No, I don't want them."

Fitzgerald smiled with relief. "I know it seems silly now, sir. But someday those moccasins—well, they'll be something to show the kids."

Curtis couldn't think of anything to say to that.

Fitzgerald stroked his knife, frowning. "But like I said, sir, they're stuck to his feet."

Curtis stared at his sergeant. "Perhaps we could soak them off after we get back to the fort," he said. "If that doesn't work, we can always cut off his feet with a saw."

Fitzgerald brightened at the suggestion. "I was afraid you might not like the idea, sir."

"Why not?" Curtis shrugged. "What difference does it make?"

Fitzgerald's big open face was utterly transparent. He was thinking: *Well, officers are peculiar.* He said, "Well, sir, I was just thinking that—"

"Never mind, Sergeant." Curtis was too weary to continue the discussion. Irony was lost on Sergeant Fitzgerald in any event.

Curtis looked down. He had been avoiding it, but now he looked down. It was a scarecrow body he saw there in the dirt, a bullet-pocketed scarecrow body. Fox Claw's shirt was gone; someone had already made off with that. The feathers had been torn from his dirty matted hair. The man had nothing left, nothing but the smile that twisted his skeleton face.

Fox Claw, damn him, was still smiling.

"Wrap him up again, Sergeant. It's time to pull out. And, Sergeant?"

"Sir?"

"I'd like for him still to be in one piece when we get to Fort Wade."

"Yes, sir." The sergeant looked puzzled.

Curtis walked away. He collected his horse from his striker and nodded to Matt Irvine to start the column. He waited until his men were ready and then took his place behind Jim at the head of the line. He fixed his eyes on Jim's dirty blanket.

The army moved out again across the empty plains.

It was a long way back to Fort Wade.

The blue column moved slowly through the silent afternoon. Only the cold kept Curtis awake in his saddle. He felt as though he could sleep for a week. Then he could get up and eat something besides beans. And then—

He shivered under his heavy coat. The sun was bright in a clear blue sky. But the sun was a winter sun and did not warm him.

The smile on Fox Claw's dead face haunted Curtis as he rode. He could not get it out of his mind. Damn it all, a man with that much lead in him should not be smiling.

He was certain that Fox Claw had seen something at the end. He had seen something out there, out in the dead grass of the empty plains.

He had seen something that Curtis could not see.

Curtis tore his eyes away from the blanket on Jim's back. He looked at the land that surrounded him, searching it, hating its total unconcern. There was nothing there for him now, nothing at all. The earth stretched away forever under the cold blue sky. The earth ignored him. The earth did not care.

It would not remember his name.

He shook his head. He was half asleep. He fumbled in his coat pocket for his pipe. He filled it and lit it easily. There was no wind. That was something.

The smoke calmed him. It cleared his brain, woke him up a little.

The trail seemed endless to him. Well, perhaps it

was. The trails that he rode had no endings, or none that he could see.

Perhaps that was his destiny, if he had a destiny. To do his best, knowing that it might not be good enough. To accept the fact that for him there would be no final victory. To want but never to have. To seek but not to find.

It was one hell of a destiny, but he was stuck with it.

He was not ashamed.

He had done his job, and perhaps a little more. He had faced up to himself. He had made the beginnings of a life with Helen, and he had made a kind of peace with Maria. He had killed a man named Fox Claw when Fox Claw had given him no other choice. He had not quit.

Tomorrow, he would be home. Fort Wade was the only home he had. He had built that post on the Canadian. He had been its only commanding officer.

How long would the fort be there, now that Fox Claw was gone?

The trail for Fox Claw was over. That trail, at least, had an ending. In some ways, Curtis thought, it had been an easier trail than the one he rode. He knew that his trail led far beyond the fort.

Curtis tapped out his pipe.

He was ready to follow that trail, wherever it led.

The column of soldiers passed within sight of Spirit Hill late that afternoon. Curtis noticed the two hills rising above the flatlands, the one higher than the other. He even saw the four twisted cedars on the south side of the taller hill.

Sleepily, he wondered if the place had a name.

It was possible, he supposed. Almost any sort of a landmark might have a name in this country. But he had never heard it, and it couldn't have been very important.

The place was barren. There was nothing there.

He glanced back at the supply wagon that carried Fox Claw's body. He saw nothing unusual.

Curtis faced forward again and pulled his coat around him against the cold. He fixed his tired eyes on Jim's dirty blanket and kept on going.

Author's Note

This is a book of fiction and does not pretend to be anything else. But the reader, if he is anything like the writer, may be curious about how much of the novel is based on fact. The best answer that I can give is to say that the general sequence of events is historical, while the principal characters are my own creation. The coming of Ishatai, the fight at Adobe Walls, the battle at Palo Duro, the hunting down of the Comanches on the Staked Plains—these are history, and I have tried not to distort the facts. But there was no Comanche named Fox Claw, as far as I know, and Dies Young is also an invented character. There was no Fort Wade on the Canadian River. Colonel Curtis, like the Twelfth Cavalry, is fictional. He is not intended to represent, however deviously, any actual cavalry officer of that period.

While it is nonsensical to burden a novel with a bibliography, it is also less than honest to decline to give credit where credit it due. This book could not have been written if other books had not been written first. I have drawn heavily on *Carbine and Lance*, by Captain W. S. Nye for many details about Fort Sill. I have made much use of materials from *Indian Fighting Army* by Fairfax Downey. For the fight at Adobe Walls, I have closely followed the account given in *The Life of Billy Dixon* by Olive K. Dixon. I have borrowed details from *The Buffalo Hunters* by Mari Sandoz, *The Indian Wars of the West* by Paul Wellman, and *The Story of Palo Duro Canyon* published by the Texas State Park Board. My friend, W. C. (Curry) Holden, who knows more of these matters than I will ever know, let me use his study in a time of need, as well as his own valuable article, "The Land," included in *A History of*

Lubbock, Part One. For the Comanches, I have relied heavily on *The Comanches: Lords of the South Plains* by Ernest Wallace and E. Adamson Hoebel, and on R. N. Richardson's *The Comanche Barrier to South Plains Settlement*.

The reader might be interested to know that the canyon of Palo Duro, some twenty-two miles from Amarillo, Texas, is now a state park. Tourists can now pitch their tents on the old Comanche camp grounds, and there is even a narrow gauge scenic railway available to carry less hardy visitors through the canyon. This presumably represents progress of a sort. A gravel road, fourteen miles from Stinnett, Texas, leads to the marked site of Adobe Walls. There is no commercial development there, and few tourists. Although the old buildings have long since disappeared, the country is still pretty much the way it used to be. If the light is right, and your imagination is good, you may still see the Comanches waiting beyond the bluff where Billy Dixon made his famous shot.

ABOUT THE AUTHOR

CHAD OLIVER was born Symmes Chadwick Oliver in Cincinnati in 1928. At the ripe old age of 14, he decided to become a Writer with a capital W. He acquired a second-hand typewriter, taught himself to type, and commenced. He moved to Crystal City, Texas, while he was still in high school. He played football and edited the school paper and the yearbook. When he was 21 years old, a student at the University of Texas, he sold his first story to Anthony Boucher of *The Magazine of Fantasy and Science Fiction*. A few years later (1952) his first novel, MISTS OF DAWN, was published.

He has written for nearly all of the science fiction magazines and wrote western fiction for such magazines as *Argosy* and *The Saturday Evening Post*. In addition to having his work chosen for many anthologies, he has contributed original fiction to such diverse collections as Harlan Ellison's AGAIN, DANGEROUS VISIONS and Joe Lansdale's BEST OF THE WEST. Some of his novels of science fiction, such as SHADOWS IN THE SUN, UNEARTHLY NEIGHBORS, and THE SHORES OF ANOTHER SEA, have achieved classic status. His western novel, THE WOLF IS MY BROTHER, won a Golden Spur Award in 1967.

Chad Oliver received his doctorate in anthropology from UCLA. He is at present Professor of Anthropology at the University of Texas at Austin, where he served for 11 years as Department Chairman. The Plains Indians are one of his major research and teaching interests, and he has also worked in East Africa.

He has been everything from a disc jockey on a show called *American Jazz* in the 1950's to Toastmaster at the North American Science Fiction Convention in 1985, but he suspects that, "If I'm remembered at all, it will probably be for my writing and I hope to do a lot more of it." He lives with his wife, Beje, who raises Arabian horses, just outside of Austin, Texas. The Olivers have two children, seven fearless chickens, two cats, one armadillo, one possum, a pair of road runners, and a fantastic squirrel that can master any bird-feeding device yet invented.

Broken Eagle, November 1864

Broken Eagle knew that the world was changing, but the name of Chivington meant nothing to him. He had never heard of the Third Colorado Cavalry. Sand Creek was just a place where The People had been told to camp.

Broken Eagle was neither young nor old as the Cheyennes counted time. He had lived for twenty summers. He was a man among The People: he had earned his name. He was not ignorant of other tribes and their ways. Arapahos were in the village, as usual. He had sat and talked sign with the Comanches, the Kiowas, and the haughty Sioux. He had learned much from those meetings. He knew that enemies could become friends, and he knew that friends had to be watched.

He was no stranger to white soldiers and treaty-makers. The intruders had covered his life like summer flies on strips of sun-drying buffalo meat. He wished that they would go away. He did not fear them, but he did not understand them. Their words were strange and twisted like smoke in the wind. They were not like other men. They clouded his mind, but there was no true hatred in his heart.

Not yet.

Broken Eagle was cold and hungry and tired. He did not show these things. That was not the way for a man. He had his horses to look after.

There was a light snowfall and he could feel the frosty breath of the Shining Mountains. The Night Sun was pale and the clear stars were visible. He sensed as well as saw the Hanging Road, *ekutsihimmiyo*, above his head. It was the path for the souls of the dead on their journey to the afterlife. He did not think about it. The Road was simply there, waiting.

The women were erecting the tipis and getting the fires going, and that was good. Broken Eagle was ready for warmth and food. A buffalo robe was too clumsy for work with the horses and his fringed leggings did not keep out the cold. His thoughts were not on war, and he was not painted.

He did not feel secure. He had never known security in his life. But there was a time for raiding and a time for rest, a time for the great buffalo hunts and a time for scattered camps and telling tales. Black Kettle had told them that Sand Creek was a protected sanctuary. Black Kettle had an American flag flying over his lodge, the first tipi that had been set up. Black Kettle had the wisdom of a Cheyenne peace chief, and old White Antelope backed his words. Who could doubt them?

Sand Creek was very low, hardly more than a trickle, but there was mud that soaked his moccasins. There were many horses in the herd and few men to check on them. Most of the warriors were out searching for scarce buffalo. The hunting had not been good and promised rations had never come.

The boys had the herd under control. There was enough water, but Broken Eagle was concerned about the grass. It was thin and wilted. There were few trees and the bark would not help much. The herd would have to be moved in a day or two, but there was little that could be done now.

He looked at all of his horses. He gave most of his attention to Coup. Coup was a bay with a white blaze on his face. He was a consecrated horse, never ridden except in war or major hunts, and he was special. Broken Eagle loved the smell of him and the intelligence in his dark liquid eyes. Coup nuzzled him and Broken Eagle stroked his ears. No two horses were alike. Some were smart and some were stupid, some were unpredictable and some were steady. Coup was a friend, and more than that. Coup was a horse a man could trust with his life.

Old men had told Broken Eagle stories of a time when The People had no horses. He believed them, but he could not imagine such a thing. It was like the story of Sweet Medicine and how he had received the Medicine Arrows in the great cave in the Black Hills. Broken Eagle could accept that as fact, but it was not a part of his own life. In the world he knew, there were horses. There *had* to be horses.

As long as he had Coup, he was a man. He could go on.

He whispered a parting word to Coup and squished back across the creek to the village. He was satisfied. The lodges were ready, glistening in the snow. It was a big camp. Counting those of Left Hand's band of Arapahos, there were more than one hundred tipis. Even with so many warriors gone on the hunt, the village must have contained around five hundred Indians. There was some power in numbers, although Broken Eagle knew that most of the people in the camp were women and children and old men.

There was woodsmoke curling in the cold still air. He could smell meat stewing in the brass kettles. The meat was elk, of course. They had nothing else except for the dogs. Broken Eagle enjoyed a tender boiled puppy as well as anyone, but the dogs were not for ordinary meals. Elk would have to do. Well, he was aware that Willow Leaf and her sisters had saved some dried slices of the Indian turnip. They knew what to do with it. The turnip would thicken and flavor the juices from the elk, making a good soup. It would fill his belly when he ladled it out with his horn spoon. It would be hot. . . .

His step quickened as he moved through the cones of the tipis. There was no need to search for his home. The arrangement was as orderly as it always was, and his lodge was in its familiar position surrounded by the tipis of Willow Leaf's relatives. He noted with approval that his round hide shield was in its proper place on the tripod by the entrance flap.

He spoke only the greeting words that courtesy required. He wanted to get inside, out of the cold. He wanted to see his wife and son, and he wanted food.

He lifted the flap and walked into his home.

The tipi was not as warm as it would be later. There had not been time for the fire to get the chill out of the hides. Nevertheless, Broken Eagle was pleased and he showed it with a smile. Willow Leaf had done well.

There was soft grass on the packed earth floor, and it was nearly dry. The willow backrests were in place and the buffalo robes were arranged properly. The parfleches were stored neatly. Broken Eagle's lance and bow were clean and ready.

He did not look directly at his wife, but he was sharply aware of her. He and Willow Leaf had only been married for slightly more than a year, and they were still shy with one another. She had cost him many horses. He knew that in former times he would not have had a wife at all at his age, and he counted himself as very lucky. Willow Leaf was beautiful to his eyes, and her supple body beneath her buckskin dress excited him.

She moved with graceful efficiency, leaving the lodge to get wooden bowls of food. The elk stew had been cooked in her mother's tipi, of course. Broken Eagle stripped down to his breechclout and turned his attention to his son.

The child gurgled happily. He was laced up on his cradleboard, hanging from a stout lodge pole, but his arms were free. He did not cry out—he already had learned that crying brought only a miserable night alone outside the tipi—but he held out his hands for his father.

Broken Eagle took the little hands and clapped them together. He kissed the boy on his forehead. He untied the cradleboard and danced around the lodge with it. He sang a soft song and he laughed. His son, who as yet had no real name, was delighted. He cooed and his brown eyes gleamed happily in the firelight.

There was no awkwardness between them. Broken Eagle adored his son, and the boy brightened whenever he saw his father. They were going to do great things together.

Broken Eagle could not wait for his son to begin walking. There was so much that he wanted to show him.

But for now, dance around the tipi! Feel the growing warmth of the fire. Drop the cradleboard and catch it just in time. Listen to the gurgles of joy. . . .

Willow Leaf returned with the bowls of hot food. She smiled at her men. Broken Eagle tried to recover a portion of his dignity, but he was flushed and happy. He replaced the cradleboard on the lodge pole and sprawled down to eat. He wolfed the thick soup. He ate very fast, both because he was hungry and because Willow Leaf would not eat until he was through.

When he finished, he propped himself against the backrest. The flood of stew in his long-empty stomach made him sleepy. His eyelids were heavy, but he watched his wife.

He liked to see her eat. She reminded him of a wild but gentle creature, a rabbit among the flowers of spring. She seemed to nibble her food. She was without haste, but she put it away. He could smell the sweetness of her body.

"It has been a long day," he said. Those were the first words he had spoken to her since morning. "I have thought much about tonight."

Willow Leaf understood him. She allowed her eyes to meet his for a moment, and then averted her gaze. "I will be ready soon," she said. Her voice was as liquid as the song from a medicine flute.

Broken Eagle waited, half dozing, as she removed the bowls and the horn spoons. He watched the small fire burn down to a bed of orange coals. As though in a dream, he saw her lift their child from the cradleboard and clean him.

She removed her dress to nurse her son. She crooned to him, a soft shadow in the uncertain light of the lodge. It took a long time, and Broken Eagle could hear the faint sound of sleet ticking against the hides of the tipi.

He must have slept a little because he was startled when she came to him under the warmth of the buffalo robe. He felt her hand on him and thrilled to her eagerness. Her breasts were wet with sweet milk.

"Willow Leaf," he said. "I cannot help myself. I am sorry."

"Do not be sorry," she whispered. "It is right. I know some things better than you."

He held back just for a moment. He knew that a Cheyenne man was supposed to remain celibate for years after the birth of his first son. That way, all of his energy was concentrated on the development of his child. He had known men who were strong enough to do that. He was not one of them. He was weak and there were hot surgings in his body. He feared for his child.

"Broken Eagle," she said. "I am your wife. The belt of chastity is gone. You are mine, and I am yours."

There were no more words. There was no thinking. There were two bodies fused into one, lost in the sheltering circle of the tipi. There were two hearts pounding and low moans of pleasure. There was a mounting of the wave, and a breaking, and a release. . . .

A suspension of time, a stillness.

The world flowed back, and Broken Eagle kissed the

shining black hair of his wife. He lifted her body and carried her to her own robe. He whispered to her and life was good.

He touched his son's sleeping head on the cradleboard and thought briefly about the night outside. Black Kettle had said nothing about sentries. There would be no need for them in this weather. It was not much of a storm, but it was enough.

And there was the American flag. That was supposed to be strong medicine.

Broken Eagle was tired but content.

He pulled his buffalo robe over him and fell into a deep sleep.

He awoke from a dream of eagles. They were soaring on splendid wings, just below the Blue Sky Space. Then they were dropping, diving with talons extended, swooping straight for his head as he crunched in the pit-blind. . . .

His eyes opened. For a long moment, he was very still. He did not realize what was happening.

There was a sharp booming crash that was not thunder. He heard a staccato cracking noise. There were ripping thuds drumming against the tipi hides.

Another explosion, and still another. Those were big guns, cannon. Many of them. There was a metallic hail that tore a shattering hole through the cold air.

Broken Eagle was looking up at a patch of gray sky. The top of his lodge was gone. It had been blown away.

He struggled to his feet. The tipi was collapsing around him. He found his lance.

"Willow Leaf," he said quickly. "Take the boy. Go for the horses if you can. Do not stop for anything. I will go first and stay between you and the horses."

He could not see clearly over the tangle of hides. He waited until she was ready with the cradleboard. He could hear shouts and screams. There was a continuous shredding crackle of rifle fire.

He moved out, his lance in his hand. There was so much confusion that he had trouble orienting himself. Some of the lodges were burning in the dawn. His people were running around like ants. There were bodies in the snow.

He saw Black Kettle. The bewildered chief was in front of his tipi. The American flag still flew. Black Kettle had hauled out a large white flag on a long pole. He was waving it back and forth. He was yelling, in English: "No, no, no! Black Kettle! American flag! Peace! No, no, no!"

His words were so much spit in the chill morning air. There were soldiers coming at them from two directions. Hundreds upon hundreds of them, all screaming and cursing. They all looked alike to Broken Eagle: drunken bearded men in winter coats.

The rifle and pistol fire was so rapid that he could not distinguish individual shots. There were yellow streaks of flame and a haze of acrid blue smoke. There was a terrible buzz of searching lead in the air. There was no place to hide. With so few warriors, there was no way to make a stand.

He pushed his wife and son toward the creek. "Down!" he said. "Crawl!"

He whirled to do what he could with his lance. Before he could even begin his charge, he was hit in the left shoulder. That was when he heard the sound he would never forget.

A wet thudding pounding noise. Bullets tearing through human flesh. So close, so near, right behind him—

He ignored his wound. He did not feel it. He turned and saw what he knew he would see.

Willow Leaf was prone in the thin snow. She was not moving. There was scarlet blood staining the whiteness around her.

Her cradleboard was strapped to her back. His son

was laced up in his cocoon. The boy's head was a bloody pulp. There was nothing left.

Broken Eagle threw himself on the bodies. He was completely stunned. He did not know that there was a battle raging around him, and he did not care.

"My son," he cried, tearing at the lashings. He found the boy's tiny hand. He twisted the fingers. They were warm but there was no life in them. He turned over the body of his wife. She was gone, cut to pieces. He kissed the blood on her mouth.

"Willow Leaf," he sobbed. "Willow Leaf."

His world had disintegrated. He lay there in shock, his own blood mixing with that of his wife and son. He willed them to live. He tried to force his life into them. He could not have said how long he tried. Long afterward, it seemed to him that he held them in his arms forever.

But they were dead. He could not bring them back.

Very slowly, Broken Eagle separated himself from Willow Leaf. He touched his child's small hand for the last time. He lurched to his feet. His blurry eyes were wild.

He picked up his lance.

Broken Eagle was both there and not there. A part of him stood in that howling chaos of the cold gray dawn and a part of him was gone.

He knew that his own wound was not mortal. He did not think of himself; he was past caring. A corner of his mind reached down into his training and told him what he should do. The remaining warriors must fight a delaying action to give the women and children a chance to escape. That was the way.

At the same time, every nerve and muscle in his body was shrieking at him. *Attack. Charge. Kill. Cut and stab and rip and slash.*

As though in the midst of a vision, he saw things with

a terrible clarity but the images were floating and disconnected. The soldiers were so many that he could not count them, flowing like dark shadows of death in their long flapping coats. They seemed to be everywhere at once, shouting and stamping and killing.

Incredibly, Black Kettle still stood. His face was a mask of unbelieving horror. He no longer tried to speak. He just waved his tattered white flag before the ruins of his lodge. The American flag had been shot from the skeleton of the tipi. It was a shapeless stain on the trampled ground.

Old White Antelope, his body twisted by many summers, was standing as straight as he could. His thin arms were folded across his chest. He made no effort to fight. He chanted his death song in a clear, resigned voice: "*Oh, I am not in this place for always. I hear the wind where there is no wind. It is only the earth and the mountains and the stars that can live forever. Oh, I am not in this place for always. . . .*"

As Broken Eagle stared, the bullets slammed into the old man's body. He was thrown back in a grotesque stumbling dance. White Antelope crumpled into a twitching lump of nothing in the dirty snow.

A grinning soldier whipped out a long-bladed knife and crouched by White Antelope's body. The soldier began to saw clumsily at the old man's scalp—

Something gave way deep inside of Broken Eagle. He could not think. He was hardly conscious and certainly not rational. He felt. He acted.

He was not aware that he had moved but he was above and behind the soldier. He kicked him in the head. The head turned and he saw strange blue eyes looking at him. Broken Eagle used his lance. There was nothing wrong with his right arm and his shoulder was good. The point of the lance drove through coat and uniform and white skin and red meat. The lance went all the way through and splintered in the half-frozen earth.

Broken Eagle tore the knife from the soldier's hand. He clamped it in his teeth. He scooped up the soldier's carbine. He picked a target with care and fired. A soldier doubled up with a slug in the stomach. Broken Eagle threw the carbine aside. It was too slow. He yanked a revolver from the lanced soldier's holster. He checked the load.

Screaming a wordless cry around the steel in his teeth, Broken Eagle charged.

There were no lines now. There were no well-defined positions. The campground was a jumble of burning tipis and howling soldiers and confused Cheyennes and Arapahos. There were piles of dead in the snow-dusted grass. Most of the dead were women and children.

Broken Eagle had no medicine and no paint. It did not matter to him. He would live or he would die. First, he would kill.

Something protected him. There was power in him. He squeezed off four shots, all of the ammunition he had, and three bullets went home. He stuck the revolver in his breechclout; there was no other way he could carry it. He took the knife out of his mouth. He was gasping for breath. The cold air and the smoke hurt his chest.

He used the knife. He slashed and stabbed and rolled until the knife was so slippery he could not get a grip on it. He dropped the knife and found a discarded saber. He picked the saber up and began to laugh.

It was the laughter of madness. Somehow, it jerked him back to a kind of sanity. He realized that he was standing on an island of death. The soldiers he could reach were dead or dying. The ones he could not reach were staying out of his range.

Broken Eagle whirled. His mind was working again. The children and the women who remained alive could have made it across the creek by now. They would need some men. He was almost the only warrior still on his feet in the burning village.

He saw Black Kettle. He was where he had been during the whole battle. Black Kettle was squatting now, rocking back and forth on his heels, crying without words. He was still trying to wave his white flag. He looked almost comical. As far as Broken Eagle could tell, the old chief had not been hit. Strange things happened in a war.

They would need Black Kettle, these that survived. Broken Eagle ran to him. He switched the saber to his weak left hand and caught Black Kettle's upper arm with his right hand. He jerked the chief to his feet, hard. This was no time for ceremony.

"Come," Broken Eagle said. "Now. We have lost enough."

Black Kettle was shaking. For just a moment, he seemed to hesitate. He looked into the eyes of Broken Eagle. He started a stumbling run in the direction of Sand Creek.

Broken Eagle did not relax his grip. "Faster," he said. He shoved the older man ahead of him.

The two men ran and did not look back.

Broken Eagle knew that they had no chance if the soldiers tried to cut them off. But the soldiers were stupid. They were not interested in the horse herd. They had what they had come after. Their minds were on whiskey and celebration.

Broken Eagle and Black Kettle slipped and splashed across the shallow puddles of the stream. Many of the horses were already gone. Those that were left were alarmed and restless. There were Indian bodies in the cold mud.

Broken Eagle isolated a mare and steadied her. It was not an easy thing to do. He lifted Black Kettle and half threw him on the horse. Black Kettle was a Cheyenne. It was child's play for him to ride bareback.

"Go," said Broken Eagle. He slapped the mare on her rump.

Broken Eagle gave a sharp whistle. He did not doubt that Coup had waited for him. He was not wrong. The bay trotted up to him expectantly. Coup was a war pony. He knew what to do.

Broken Eagle mounted. His wound was hurting him now and his chest was greasy with blood that refused to dry. He still held the saber but he could clutch Coup's mane.

"No, old friend," he whispered as Coup instinctively turned toward the smoking village. "Not this time."

He guided his reluctant horse away. He rode only a short distance until he topped a rise. He pulled Coup to a halt.

With the sun burning through the mists of morning, Broken Eagle turned and looked back at what had been his village.

He was too far away to recognize individuals but he could see what was going on. He could see all too well.

The soldiers had gone crazy. They were madmen prowling and dancing and looting through the flames and the ruins. It seemed to Broken Eagle that there was one detachment of troops that was held in check by its officers. He could not be sure but it looked as though these soldiers were not participating in the carnage.

But the others.

Scalping, yes, but that was the least of it. The soldiers swarmed over the bodies of the dead men, hacking off their genitals and waving them in the air. Bayonets were driven into lifeless corpses. The bodies of women were kicked and stabbed. Breasts were cut off for souvenirs. Infants were tossed up high, their arms and legs flopping, and caught on slashing sabers.

No Indian lived in the camp of Black Kettle. It was a village of horror.

Broken Eagle watched as long as he could. There was a sickness in him but he did not close his eyes. He forced himself to think of Willow Leaf. He made himself imagine that it was his son impaled on sabers and bayonets. He thought of friends and relatives. He wanted to remember this day.

When he could stand it no longer, he urged Coup into a rapid walk. He did not look back again.

He was a nearly naked man on a war horse that could not understand. He had lost his world: his wife, his son, his home, his shield, his bow, his lance, his warm buffalo robes. He had an empty revolver in his breechclout and a rust-red saber in his hand. He had blood on his naked chest and his eyes were as cold as the blue ice of winter. His heart was a stone.

He did not slouch and he did not give way to pain. He held himself erect on Coup's back, flowing with his horse. He stared at nothing and his face was a frozen mask.

He drank the bittersweet air of morning.

Sand Creek had taken much from Broken Eagle. But it had given him something in return.

Broken Eagle had found hate.